You've Got Something Coming

Jonathan Starke

You've Got Something Coming

Jonathan Starke

Black Heron Press
Post Office Box 614
Anacortes, Washington 98221
www.blackheronpress.com

You've Got Something Coming is a work of fiction. All characters that appear in this book are products of the author's imagination. Any resemblance to persons living or dead in entirely accidental.

ISBN (print): 978-1-936364-32-9
ISBN (ebook): 978-1-936364-33-6

Black Heron Press
Post Office Box 614
Anacortes, Washington 98221
www.blackheronpress.com

You've Got Something Coming

HORATIO HORSFALL CHILDREN'S HOME
OF KLAKANOUSE, WISCONSIN

Trucks waited outside the children's home. He had on a dark workman's coat and carried two used hearing aids in his pocket. He'd been sitting on the ground for a half hour with his back to the bricks, opening and closing his hands, looking at his knuckles worn down from all the boxing.

The front door swung open. The late-night dishwasher looked around.

Trucks put his gloves back on, stood, and walked over through the dark.

The dishwasher told him how to find the room.

Trucks nodded and walked on. He zipped his coat down. Then he zipped it back up. He was nervous. He'd lived in places like this as a kid. They all smelled the same, like faint lemon and must. There were nightlights in half-moons lining the long hall. They blinked as he moved forward. Door after door.

He stopped outside the room. What he was doing here would change everything. He knew that. All the money he had now was in his pocket. Thirty dollars from the fight he'd taken that night. He got clipped behind the ear with a phantom hook. Never saw it coming. It wobbled him, and he'd reached for the ropes and fell. The sharp headache, the blur, the hot lights. He didn't get up for the count. Someone from the crowd threw a beer on him. Trucks sat drenched and sticky while the ref came over, tugged on his eyelids with his thumbs.

Trucks opened the door and walked over to the corner bed. He got down on a knee. Moonlight cut through the window. With all that snow, it was nearly blue outside. He hoped she wouldn't see his busted face.

"There are no stars, Pepper Flake." He didn't finish the quote. He couldn't remember how it ended. It was something an old boxing trainer used to say to him. Trucks didn't know why it came to him now.

Claudia was asleep. Trucks watched the ebb of her chest. Her fluttering eyelids. He ran his thumb over her eyebrow the way so many cut men had done for him, closing his gashes, sweeping away the dark blood.

His little girl's birthday was today.

Trucks gently squeezed Claudia's bicep. She squirmed and blinked out of confusion. She recognized him soon after, though she looked uncertain if he was an apparition or the truth.

"It's me," Trucks whispered. He didn't want to wake the other girls.

Claudia turned from him. Trucks sat on the edge of the bed and patted her back. Claudia pulled away and scooted to the wall.

"I told you I'd come for you. Didn't you believe me?"

Claudia didn't answer. Trucks remembered the used hearing aids and pulled them out of his pocket. He looked down—two russet pea pods on his palm. He'd bought them at a thrift store after he found out from the dishwasher that Claudia was losing her hearing. Trucks knew the overrun children's home wouldn't cover it.

Claudia looked over her shoulder.

Trucks moved closer. He held up the hearing aids. Claudia rolled away again.

"I cleaned them," he said. Trucks always carried a sachet of antibacterial wipes. An obsessive habit. He tapped her on the shoulder until she turned toward him. She crossed her arms over her chest and kept her eyes shut. Trucks clicked the hearing aids on and hooked one to each ear and inserted the earmolds.

"Check," he said.

Claudia shook her head. Trucks raised the volume dial of each hearing aid.

"Cross, hook, hook," he said.

Claudia shook her head again. Trucks turned the dials up.

"How about now, Pepper Flake?"

Claudia opened her eyes.

"You could have maybe died," she said. "You were gone forever."

Trucks looked at the floor. "You know I'm not really the dying kind. I told you that."

"Can you promise again?"

"I can promise."

"Then promise. And don't die."

Trucks looked in her eyes. Then he looked at his hands. He made a fist with his left and rubbed his right across his wounded knuckles. Then he looked out the window. The clouds had shifted. His face was so visible against the harsh moonlight.

"You're all hurt again," Claudia said. "They won't let me go home if you don't stop. You promised."

Claudia turned back to the wall. The boxing wasn't the whole story, but she didn't know that. Trucks thought he could hear sniffles. She was crying into her wrists.

"And you missed my birthday," she said.

"It's barely past midnight. We can still call it your birthday. I've got a gift for you outside. A really special one. They said I could give it to you if I came at night so it wouldn't make the other kids jealous."

"You're lying," she said into the wall.

"Honest," he said.

Claudia rolled back. "I don't believe you."

"It's true."

Trucks held out his hand. Claudia was reluctant. Still, she threw off the covers and sat up. Trucks noticed how much longer her hair was now, how the curls had grown thicker in his absence. Six months had been too long.

"Come outside," he said.

"I don't know."

"Trust me."

"Maybe."

Trucks got up from the bed and looked out the window into the cobalt night. A thick birch covered in snow.

Trucks turned to Claudia. He offered his hand again. She took it, and he pulled her to her feet. Then he picked her coat from the bedpost and she put it on. Her winter boots were by the bed, and she slipped into them and loosely tied the laces. Trucks bent down and tightened them.

"Let's keep quiet and not say anything else until we're outside, okay?"

Claudia nodded.

They'd have to forget about rifling through drawers for spare clothes. It was time to go.

Trucks walked to the bedroom door. Claudia followed a few steps, then stopped. She glanced at the three girls, asleep in their beds. Then she walked over to their bedsides, touched each girl differently—on the ankle, the forehead, the hand. Then she came out of the room with a sad face. Trucks tried to hold Claudia's hand, but she pulled away. Together they walked down the long hall, past the blinking half-moons and ever closer to the cold world that would reveal itself just beyond the front door.

HITCHING OFF 90

They were lying in the bed of a fast-moving pickup under a woolen tarp for dead cattle. The tarp went up to their necks. It smelled awful. After a while, they got used to it.

"We'll stay together this time?" Claudia asked.

"Yeah," Trucks said.

They watched the pale night sky, still lit from the snow.

"Till the end?" she asked.

"Till the end," he said.

They looked up into the moving dark.

"They won't find us where we're going. Nobody will."

"Yeah?"

"Nevada's way out there. We'll keep our distance. We'll be all right."

"What's it like there?"

Trucks had Claudia against his side and pulled her closer. His hands stung. He'd given her his thick gloves. They were too big on her, and they'd had a nice laugh about it. Trucks and Claudia had walked to a highway junction where the old road met the interstate, and they'd stood in the deep snow with their thumbs out. When Claudia started shivering, Trucks picked her up and held her, his knuckles and temple aching from the fight the night before. Then it was just him holding his sleeping girl with a cold thumb out.

The pickup roared and rattled on I-90, past the Dells and Lacrosse and into Minnesota territory. Could he smell the frozen-over Mississippi? No. Surely not.

"Maybe you should sleep some more," he said.

"If you tell me about Nevada I'll maybe fall asleep."

Trucks gave her a squeeze.

"Is that where Mama is? Waiting in Nevada?" she asked.

Trucks didn't say anything. He opened and closed his fist. Ran his knuckles back and forth against the tarp to feel that burn.

"Is she there?" Claudia asked.

"She's not in Nevada, Pepper Flake." Trucks looked at Claudia. "You should close your eyes. Try to get some rest before he drops us off."

"Where's he dropping us?"

"I don't know. He said maybe Sioux Falls. It's in South Dakota. Do you know where that is?"

Claudia looked at her big-gloved fingers. She counted on them as if it would help her identify where South Dakota was.

"No," she said. "Do we have to hitch there? I don't wanna hitch anymore. It's freezing."

Claudia swung a leg over Trucks. She pulled in closer to collect his warmth. He knew it was about survival, but it still made him feel good. He was barely even thinking about the boxing. Wasn't counting back combinations in his mind, picturing footwork, or trying to see his punches as lines drawn by invisible string.

"We'll take a break somewhere and get you warm. But we have to keep moving. We always have to keep moving until it's safe. Okay?"

Claudia sighed. He felt it on his ribs.

"Tell me okay."

"Okay," she said.

The pickup rumbled. The tailgate clanked. The driver was an old rancher who'd gone to Milwaukee to purchase vintage rifles and scopes from an antique gun show. Trucks felt fortunate he'd picked them up. Figured it was probably the way he saw Trucks with his girl in one arm, her pink cheek on his shoulder, his busted hand stuck out, that stomach-pit desperation in his eyes.

"How are your hearing aids holding up? You seem to be doing pretty good."

"They pinch my ears. But they're okay, I guess." Claudia tapped her left hearing aid. "This one's blurry."

"You mean *staticky*. And maybe I can get it fixed once we get to Nevada. I don't know what I can do about the pinching. It was the smallest I could find."

"I'm scared the other kids are gonna make fun of me."

Trucks could feel her sharp breathing against him.

"I really am," she said.

Trucks held her tight. "The hell they will."

HALLOWELL DRUG AND SUNDRIES

Trucks and Claudia sat on a palate of stacked charcoal bags inside the store. It was early morning and the store was dead. Claudia kicked her heels against the bags. Trucks blew into his hands.

"I froze out there for you," he said.

"But you didn't even turn into a snowman," she said.

"Good one," he said.

Claudia had taken off her coat and the too-big gloves. Trucks realized then, as if for the first time, that she was wearing pajamas. A purple long-sleeve top and matching bottoms, the arms and legs cuffed pink. It stood out to him now under all the fluorescents. How cold she must have been out there on the road. What it would have done to her fragile skin.

Claudia pointed at her hearing aids and made a sad face.

"They're too big," she said. "The other kids are gonna call me names."

"What would they call you?"

"I don't know. Mean stuff. Like Dooty Ears 'cause the hearing phones are brown." She pointed to her left ear. "And this one's still blurry."

"Staticy. And you mean hearing aids."

Claudia pulled out her left hearing aid and handed it to Trucks. He didn't know what to do with it. He put it up to his ear and shook it. Then he blew on it. He flipped it on and off. Rolled the volume dial up and down, then put it back where it seemed to work best for her.

"Give it a try now," he said.

He hooked the hearing aid back on Claudia's ear and inserted the earmold.

Claudia gave him a half-hearted thumbs-up.

"Still not so great?"

Claudia shrugged. Then she put his oversized gloves back on. Trucks smiled. Claudia leaned way back and stared at the ceiling. All those beams and white light.

"What are those?" she asked.

Trucks looked up. "Those what?"

"The triangles on the roof. There, there, there, there. And there." She pointed all along the ceiling.

"Rafters."

"What for?"

"They keep the building from falling down. You feeling warm yet?"

"Why would it fall?"

"I don't know. Wear and tear. Avalanche. Tornados."

"I think it'd be fun to play in a tornado."

Trucks laughed.

"And to swing on the raffers."

"Rafters."

"Rafters."

"Good."

Claudia often stunned him with the simplest things. Her phrasings. A look. Her nuances. He was used to the language of bobs and weaves and slips and counter-punches. The movement was the language, his fire marked his words.

"So, you warm now, Pepper Flake?"

"Yeah. I like it in here. I like looking at the raf-*ters*."

Trucks looked up again. "Think of them like the ribs of the building. Like what you got here." Trucks poked at Claudia's ribs, and she giggled. "Come on, Poopy Ears, we need to get you some things."

Trucks got down from the charcoal bags and held Claudia's hand as she jumped. He pulled out his sachet of antibacterial wipes and offered her the pack.

"I don't wanna," she said.

"You gotta keep clean. How many times do I have to tell you?"

"A thousand."

"Just take a wipe and do it."

"No."

Trucks grabbed Claudia's sleeves and rolled them up her forearms. She huffed but didn't pull away. He wiped vigorously from her wrists to her fingertips. One arm, then the other.

"See. Not so bad."

"It smells like Mama."

"Shush."

Trucks grabbed Claudia's coat and threw it over his shoulder. Claudia bit into the fabric of her glove. He led them up and down the aisles until he found the toothbrushes. There were lots to choose from. Trucks went for the knockoff brand at forty-nine cents a brush. He grabbed an adult toothbrush, a children's toothbrush, and an eight-ounce bar of shampoo-soap. He'd cut it into quarters later on.

"Not again," Claudia said.

"What?"

"It makes my hair gross." Claudia held up a bunch of curls.

"When I was growing up, they gave us apple cider vinegar and lard soap. We're getting two for one here. It's lime. Look." Trucks held up the bar. "Double-size bar. Twice as much for the same money."

"Yuck. Pick one with a good flavor. I don't wanna smell like lime."

"Fine." Trucks put the bar back. "And you mean *scent*, not flavor. So what about this one? It's chocolate-raspberry. Do people wanna smell like that all day?"

"I do."

"Then grab that one or go through the others and pick one you like."

Claudia squatted and sifted through the soap, looking for different scents and calling them out. Cinnamon, mango, oatmeal, orange. Trucks stepped back. He watched her sift. This little girl he'd made. How could it strike him so suddenly, as if it had just happened in that moment, as if he hadn't been there years ago to palm her ribs with his entire hand? His left. The one that had levied such force in the ring. The one that was waning now with age. Forty-one years of pick up, pull, push, parry, pivot, punch.

And her. Boom. As if from the sky.

"I want this one." Claudia held a mint bar under his nose. Pulled him back like all those ripe-smelling salts.

"We'll smell like Christmas mints." He grabbed the bar from her and held it in one hand with the toothbrushes.

"Baking soda next. Then we need to get some food some-where. How are you? Hungry?"

"Can't we do real toothpaste?"

"There's nothing wrong with baking soda and water. It'll make your teeth strong."

"But we had real toothpaste at the home. I want the real stuff. Baking soda's gross, and it goes gooey in the water." She crossed her arms.

"I gave in on the soap."

"Real stuff."

"No."

"Come on!"

"I said no."

"Yes."

"You turned into a real pain, you know that?"

"They never said I was a pain at the home."

"Well, you're back with me now."

"The home didn't leave me."

Trucks grabbed Claudia's arm real tight above the elbow. "They took you from me. They *took you*. I didn't leave. I'd never leave you. You got it?"

"Ouch. It hurts. Let go, let go, let go."

Trucks let go, and Claudia ran down the aisle and tur-ned the corner. He breathed deep. What had the therapist at the free clinic said all those years ago? Count it back? Find a mental sanctuary? Imagine a flock of birds flying over a pond? Whatever. Now wasn't the time to get his head right.

Trucks took off down the aisle. He found her sitting cross-legged in front of a display of antifreeze jugs.

Trucks inched down next to Claudia and sat beside her.

He put the toothbrushes and soap on the ground. Leaned his head back against the cool jugs. They sat for a while like that. Listening to each other's breathing, eyes closed. Occasionally they'd hear the footfalls of customers trickling in, the squeaky wheels of shopping carts. Time passed like that. It was nice in its way.

"Life gets complicated, Pepper Flake," Trucks finally said. "Nobody was ever telling me to take good paths. I didn't even know they existed. And nobody ever promised to stick around or ice my wounds or sew my cuts. Could I have made myself into something more than a boxer? Made cash in any other way but with hooks and headshots? I guess. But I was raised in those homes too. I know that long walk. I know that hard bed. I know those shared dressers and made-and-lost bonds and people picking on you. And listen, you need to know the way it crushed me when they took you."

Trucks looked up at the ceiling. Something had caught his eye. A bird had flown at an angle between the slanted rafters. It looked like a plover.

Then he said, "Sometimes people just go. My parents abandoned me to a shelter outside Milwaukee. I never knew why. I wondered. And I'm sure you wonder things, too, like about your mama. And I'll tell you about her someday. I'll give you all the hard answers. But what I want you to know right now is that some people are born with a wild wind inside them that carries them to distant places. I guess it's because they're sad about who they are. They're sad about what they don't have. They're sad about all those empty, broken places. And maybe they go off somewhere that the voice doesn't carry, and we'll never hear anything from them again. No return. No receipt. Like they're trapped in the bottle of themselves with a glued-down cork. And they just don't…they don't know how to make a life out of two hands and a heart. But that's all I've ever had. Look at these, you know? I've got cuts and bruises and scar tissue for miles. But now I've got you again, and our horizon's lit up. Just think of it that way, Pepper Flake. We'll just go and go and go and rip through that big powdery sky together. And there won't be no you or me. There will always be you *and* me. Us. No matter what. And don't forget that. Even if I yell or you yell or we knock each other back into sense. This is what we have. This is what we do. We go and we go together."

Trucks's throat was dry. His palms sweaty. He opened and closed his left hand, the one he'd broken three times. Twice on hooks, once on an uppercut. He looked for the plover in the rafters.

Claudia slid off one of the big gloves and took his hand. The touch jolted him. She pulled back, looked at his roughed-up face, and reached out again. She clasped his hand and leaned her head on his shoulder. Trucks cried then. He did it silently. And the crying was slight, nearly imperceptible, so she wouldn't hear. He didn't know what his little girl might make of it.

Trucks pulled Claudia into an empty aisle before they got to the checkout. He looked around—no staff in sight. He put a finger to his lips, unzipped her coat, and stuffed all their items inside except for one toothbrush. Then he zipped up her coat, gave Claudia the toothbrush, and led her to the register, where the tired clerk smiled and checked them out, saying nothing.

Once outside, Trucks dropped to a knee and emptied the items from Claudia's coat into a plastic bag the clerk had given them for the toothbrush. Then he zipped Claudia's coat to her chin and buttoned her throat flaps. Pulled her hood on. Said, "That's not normally something I'd do back there, but we're in need right now. Stealing isn't exactly stealing when you're in need like us. Understand?"

"I don't know," Claudia said.

"I can explain it better later," Trucks said. "Let's just call it 'need borrowing' for now. Deal?"

"But—"

"Deal?"

"Okay."

Trucks stood.

"Hey, look," he said.

They looked at the horizon. The sun rose in waves of blues and pinks and reds. Like it was coming out of a birth of paint. They were quiet for minutes. The chilling South Dakota wind whipped on. Then Trucks took her hand, and they got to walking.

BREAKFAST AT THE KOOL FUEL CAFE

Trucks had seen the Kool Fuel gas station when the old rancher dropped them off in the Hallowell parking lot. What he'd noticed, really, was a beige mechanical pony sitting outside on a dark pole. It faced the barren field beside the gas station. Looked like it had been itching for so many years to blaze across the plains. He knew it might be tough to catch another ride for a while, so he could entertain Claudia with the pony while he tried to hitch.

They walked inside the gas station. Trucks grabbed two small paper cups next to the soda machine. They took off their coats and sat at one of the glued-to-the-wall tables near the open case of rolling hot dogs and sausages. Donuts under glass. Coffee pots and sugar packets and dried spills from hours before. Trucks set the paper cups on the table. Claudia picked up the cups and put them over her eyes like binoculars.

"I can't see anything out there, cappy captain," she said.

"Maybe they're not in focus. Did you turn the focus knob?"

"Yeah."

"Hm. Strange. It must be all that thick fog rolling over the plains."

Claudia put the cups top-down on the table.

"Other side," Trucks said.

She turned the cups over. "What's it matter?"

"Germs," he said.

Trucks took the sachet out of his pocket.

"Hands," he said.

"Again?"

Trucks nodded. "Take those off."

Claudia took off her gloves. Trucks handed her an antibacterial wipe.

"That smell," she said.

"Get cleaned up."

Claudia slowly rubbed the damp wipe over her hands. Trucks raised an eyebrow. Claudia made a face and scrubbed fast like she was trying to start a fire. Trucks wanted to stay stern, but he couldn't help laughing. Claudia giggled and tossed the used wipe on the table. Trucks picked it up and cleaned his hands. Then he opened their plastic sack and pulled out a can of beans, a package of shredded cheese, and a skinny metal can opener. He opened the can of beans and dumped half into one of the cups, half in the other.

"Open that bag of cheese, and dump some in each of the cups," he said.

Claudia picked up the bag, bit into the corner, and jerked her head to rip it open. She poured too much cheese in one of the cups.

"Try to keep it even, knucklehead."

"I *am* trying, bruiseity brains."

Trucks knocked on his head. "Still working, at least." Although his head hadn't stopped aching from the fight.

Claudia added more cheese, and Trucks went over to the counter and grabbed two plastic spoons. He came back and put them on the table and sat down.

Claudia grabbed a spoon and tried to dig in right away. Trucks held his spoon out to her.

"To the road," he said.

Claudia clicked her spoon against his.

"To the road," she said.

Halfway through her cup, Trucks stood and put on his coat.

"I'll be right out that window, okay? See over there at the end of the building?"

Claudia looked sad.

"I'm not going anywhere far. I'm not leaving, promise. I'm just going to the end of the building, right outside. Sit here. Don't go anywhere. Don't talk to anyone. If anyone tries to talk to you, tell them to go away. Say something like, 'My dad's right there. He's got a gun, and he'll blow your ugly face off.'" Trucks smiled.

"Sounds kinda mean."

"Just a joke."

"Yeah."

"Should we make it nicer?"

"Yeah."

"Okay. I'll figure out something nicer when I get back. And then we're gonna try out our new toothbrushes in the bathroom."

Claudia made a face.

Trucks walked away, reached the door, paused with his hand on the glass, then came back.

"Hey you," he said.

"Hey you," she said.

Claudia looked up at him, her face at an angle. She looked like her mother just then. Trucks leaned down and hugged her tight. Some of the beans spilled over the side of the cup in her hands. Trucks grabbed a napkin and wiped the table. He picked up all the trash. Then he went through the front door and pitched the garbage in a barrel between the gas pumps before walking to the end of the building.

Claudia set her cup down when she was finished eating. She rattled her spoon around inside the cup. Then she rested her chin on her fists and stared at the blank wall ahead. Outside, Trucks pulled his coat tighter to fend off the cold. He was down on his knees in the snow, furiously scrubbing the beige mechanical horse with antibacterial wipes.

THE QUARTER PONY RIDES

It was late morning. Trucks stood at the edge of the gas station parking lot where the exit met the highway. Claudia was in the distance behind him sitting on the beige mechanical pony. Its stand was painted navy blue and said "Ride the Champ" in faded newsprint lettering. The paint was chipping. The horse was chipping. Somehow the beige hadn't gotten too bleached out over all those years in the sun.

Trucks thought about Claudia, what a good girl she was. She had to be sick of that pony by now. Each time the ride ended, Claudia called out for him, and Trucks walked back from the road and popped in another quarter. After a while, he didn't have any quarters left, but he asked her to stay there on the lifeless pony anyway. It was better like that. She was protected from the cold wind as long as she kept against the building.

For Trucks, the time went like this:

Thumb out. Car passed. Driver ignored him.

Thumb out. Car passed. Driver ignored him.

Thumb out. Car passed. Driver pointed ahead, mouthed *sorry*, drove on.

He often looked over his shoulder at Claudia. It had been six months since he had to be responsible for her. Now she was sitting backward on the pony. Earlier she'd gotten down

and looked at its belly. He saw her rubbing the underside of
the pony and speaking to it. He couldn't make out the words
because of the harsh wind, but he could see her mouth moving. Occasionally he heard a fraction of her soft voice.

Trucks had put their supply sack on the ground near the
pony to keep his hands free. Whenever someone pulled up
to a gas pump, Trucks would walk over and ask for a ride.
People seemed afraid of his bruised face. Uptight about the
black-and-purple markings and one of the dried cuts at the
edge of his eye. Some held the fuel pump spout between
themselves and Trucks as he approached. Pointing it at him
like a gun. They all took defensive postures. He'd be kind.
They'd say no for various reasons. Had to get to work. Going
the other direction. Just heading down the road a few exits.
Didn't believe in picking up hitchers. Things like that. When
he told them about his daughter and pointed her out on the
pony, they'd dart their eyes between him and her. He could
tell they thought it was one of those sympathy scams. Like
they'd get a ways down the road and he'd take them by the
throat while she stuck a knife to their ribs.

Trucks felt desperate. The highway was empty and gray
and cold. Cars weren't passing much on this barren stretch.

Had it been an hour? Trucks turned from the road and
walked over to Claudia. She was off the pony now and had
her face against the gas station window.

"Anything interesting?" Trucks asked.

"Not really." She kept looking through the window.

"You warm enough?"

"I'm fine."

"You having fun watching the store?" Trucks glanced at

the road.

"I saw a guy buy your tickets."

"My tickets?"

"The tickets you let me scratch with pennies."

"Oh."

For a time Trucks wasn't making any money, and he'd tried to change his luck with scratch-off tickets. But it brought him nothing, and over the years he went broke again and again. Too many hours at the gym and too many overdue notices. His life had consisted of late payments and nonpayments. Some "concerned" citizen had seen the low way he was living with Claudia in that dump of a rowhouse down by the tracks. Probably somebody he'd wronged. Somebody who had it in for him. So that somebody called the state. Then the state showed up. Claudia was taken from him again and again. Put in a home. Returned. Put in a different home. Returned. Soon the state had had enough, citing his past indiscretions of street fighting, his long arrest record, his inability to pay the bills, to keep a job, to quit taking beatings for cash and find "healthy, gainful employment." That's what they'd called it in their letters. Six months ago they took Claudia and said it'd be for good. It tore up Trucks. But he used the anger and sorrow to fuel a plan. He took every available fight in the city, regardless of weight class, and accepted even the smallest fight purses. Trucks barely ate. He dropped twenty pounds. But over the months he paid off his overdue bills and claims and interest. And still the state denied his custody requests. Said the appeals process would go on and on, and Trucks was afraid if he didn't do something soon he'd lose his girl. He'd been on the outs with the state from the get-go and only saw one option—to fight the only way he knew how. All knuckle and bone and grit and heart. So he got connected with the late-night dishwasher at the Horatio Horsfall Children's Home through a local bookie in Klakanouse. The dishwasher would do his best to find out how Claudia was doing and relay the info. And when the time came, the dishwasher snuck him in, and Trucks got his girl back. He was left with thirty dollars, and that speck of money had to carry him and Claudia halfway across the country to Nevada, where he was told the casino boxing market was solid. And sometimes he thought maybe he could start a different kind of life that was better for his girl. Be a trainer. A cutman. A coach. Anything but what he was. That he could walk away from the ring and the beatings. The late-night stitches and pulsing knuckles. He told himself this.

"I thought I could snag a ride alone, but I'm gonna need your help on this one," Trucks said to Claudia.

She pried herself from the window and looked at him. "Told ya."

"You did."

"So what do I do?"

"It's gonna be pretty chilly out there. You'll need to have your big-girl pants on."

Claudia pulled out the waistband of her pajama bottoms, then let it go so it snapped against her stomach. She laughed.

"Good. Now pop that hood on."

Claudia put her hood on.

Trucks got down on a knee and secured the hood. Then he picked up the Hallowell sack in his left hand, the one he'd broken so many times, and opened his right arm for Claudia to swoop in. "I'll lift you up and carry you out to the shoulder of the road. Keep your face turned into me. Remember, if we get a ride, don't say anything about who we are or where we're from. Let me do the talking. If they ask any questions, look to me first before you answer. Never say your real name. Never talk about Klakanouse. We're not from Wisconsin. We've never been there. Okay?"

Claudia looked at Trucks, then all around. She fidgeted with the strings of her coat. "Okay," she said. "But where are we from?"

"Good question." Trucks thought a moment. "Let's say Georgia. It sounds nice. I bet it's warm there now."

"Georgia." Claudia tried it on.

Then she walked into his open arm. Trucks picked her up and stood, feeling the weight of her. Trucks could half see into the store and half see himself reflected in the glass with Claudia in his arms, the brute plains behind him.

He breathed in deep, turned, and walked past the fuel pumps. The wind picked up even more after that. He paused at the edge of the highway. There was plenty of room for somebody to stop. A nearly deserted road. Shouldn't be a problem.

"Hanging tight?" Trucks asked. He liked feeling the weight of his girl. She had her cheek against his shoulder. She nodded into his body.

"Think warm thoughts. This is what they call bitter cold, Pepper Flake."

Claudia mumbled into his coat. He could feel the buzz of her breath against him.

HEADING FOR KADOKA

"It's really against my nature, but I saw your little girl," the woman said. She had on a silk blouse, tight black pants, white pumps, and pearl earrings. She wore a gold necklace that sparkled against the occasional rays of the peeking sun. The woman was driving twenty miles an hour over the speed limit. They were back on I-90, still heading west. Trucks and Claudia were sitting in the backseat of the woman's nice sedan, their sack of supplies between them.

"We're grateful you did." Trucks patted Claudia's leg.

The woman tapped the steering wheel.

"We're from Georgia," Claudia offered.

Trucks gave her a look.

"Oh?" the woman said. "I toured the university in Athens once. Pretty little college town. Have you been?"

Trucks didn't know Georgia at all. Maybe he should have suggested a state he'd been to.

"Yeah, a few times. A pretty little college town, like you said. But we're small-town folks. We live on the other side of the state."

"I'm a small-town girl myself," the woman said. "From Kadoka, where I'm headed. But I've been living in Sioux Falls for about fifteen years now. Kadoka's tiny in comparison, nothing much to do."

"Why are you going there?" Claudia asked.

Trucks squeezed her arm. She was breaking his rules.

"I've been running back and forth to see my sister," the woman said, looking at Claudia in the rearview. Then she looked at Trucks and said, "She's been sick for a while. I'm practically paying rent at a hotel up there. She has a small efficiency that barely suits one, so I get my own room to give her privacy and, honestly, just to have a breather and my own space."

"I'm sorry about your sister," Trucks said.

"Thanks. I'm just hoping she'll pull through."

"So it's serious?"

"Follick's Disease. It has to do with low blood cell counts and the inability to regenerate cells. It's depressing to talk about, you know?"

"I'm sorry," Trucks said.

"Thanks." The woman looked in the rearview at Trucks. "So, speaking of traumas, I was curious about your face. May I ask what happened?"

Trucks felt his forehead and temple. The wounds still tender to the touch.

"I'm a boxer," he said. Like there was nothing else he had ever been or could ever be.

"Ah," the woman said. "You must have had a fight recently?"

"Just the other day."

"How did it go?"

"I did all right. Took a bit of a beating, I guess. I had a lot on my mind. If you wanna fight well, you can't be thinking of anything but the man across from you. My movement was off. My breathing was off. My mind was somewhere else."

Trucks reached over and swept some of Claudia's hair behind her ear.

"I bet that makes for a long night," the woman said. She smiled. Trucks could see it in the rearview.

"That's for sure," Trucks said.

"You ever been hit before?" Claudia asked the woman.

"Jesus," Trucks said. "I'm really sorry. She's never like this."

"Why can't I ask questions?" Claudia said.

"It's okay," the woman said. "It's a perfectly fine question, but it's not one I want to answer. Is that fair?"

"Yeah," Claudia said.

Trucks couldn't tell if he was overreacting. He'd told Claudia what to say and not to say to draw as little attention to them as possible. Yeah, his face was messed up and they were an odd hitching pair, but what could he do about it?

"Can I sit with you?" Claudia asked.

The woman didn't answer right away. "If it's all right with your father, sure," she finally said. "I could use some front-seat company."

Trucks didn't like the idea, but he could see the way Claudia was drawn to the woman.

"Sure, okay," Trucks said.

The woman grabbed her purse from the passenger seat and put it on her lap. "She can just come between the seats. I've got the wheel steady. No traffic."

Trucks took Claudia's hand. She bent down and stepped between the seats. Trucks guided her forward. Claudia plopped down in the passenger seat.

"Buckle," Trucks said.

Claudia clicked the belt in place. The woman moved her purse from her lap to the floor in front of Claudia's feet. Claudia stared at the woman. Watched her delicate hands on the wheel. Her bright nail polish.

"I like your smell," Claudia said.

"Thanks," the woman said. "It's called Purely Passion, made from fruits and flower petals from South America. It's supposed to make men desire you, but I don't know."

She laughed. Claudia giggled.

"Here," the woman said, pointing to her purse. "Dig around. It's in there somewhere."

Claudia leaned forward and picked up the purse. She sifted through it. Then she pulled out the woman's pocketbook and opened it.

"June," Claudia said, looking at the woman's driver's license. "Like the month."

"Ugh, just ignore the hideous photo," June said.

Trucks leaned forward and looked at the driver's license. He thought she looked surprisingly pretty in the photo. Her blond hair was bright and straight, her blue eyes striking. He'd tried not to stare at her much because he didn't want her to feel even more self-conscious or defensive than she probably already did.

"Well, I'm June. I feel rude now. I should have introduced myself from the start. You're my first hitchhikers, so I don't know the etiquette. Plus, I was nervous."

"You're doing fine," Trucks said.

June smiled. Trucks returned to the backseat.

"How about you two?"

"Us?" Trucks asked.

"Yeah, what should I call you? Hitcher One and Hitcher Two?"

"Oh." Trucks paused. "Now I'm being rude. I'm Ezzard. That's Pearl there, rifling through your purse."

"Yeah, Pearl," Claudia said.

"It's nice to meet you both. Ezzard! What a fascinating name."

It was the first name that popped in his head. Ezzard Charles was his favorite classic boxer. A real ring technician. Trucks had learned a lot from reading about Charles's movement and punching techniques. Like how to throw a jumping hook with his lead left hidden behind the jab. It was something he'd tried to mimic in the ring.

"It's one of those family names," Trucks said. "My grandfather's middle name. It gets passed down to one or another of the kids. Lucky me, huh?"

"Very unique," June said.

"So I guess you picked up one of those Ezzard boys," Trucks said.

"Sure looks like it," June said. "And, like I said, this isn't normal for me. I've never picked up hitchhikers before, but I saw you carrying your daughter on your shoulder, and something made me pull over. I felt an incredible rush when I stepped on the brake."

"I know what you mean," Trucks said.

"Plus, you're so adorable," June said to Claudia. "Those curls! I just want to touch them."

"You can," Claudia said. She grabbed a handful of curls

and held them out toward June.

June reached over and ran her delicate fingers through Claudia's hair. Her face glowed with June's touch.

"How far do you think we are from your hometown?" Trucks asked.

"Kadoka's probably three hours away still," June said.

"That's a good distance."

"Yeah. I've made this drive so many times over the past months. It's nice to finally have some company."

Trucks wondered how such a kind and good-looking woman like that didn't have company on her trips.

Claudia put the pocketbook away and finally got to the perfume. She turned the onion-shaped bottle in her hand. Sniffed it. Flicked the little pump.

"Can I try some?" Claudia asked.

June looked in the rearview.

"Sure," Trucks said. He hadn't seen Claudia so taken with someone before.

"Just spray a tiny bit on the insides of your wrists and pat them together," June said.

Claudia squeezed the pump a few times. "Oops. A lot came out."

June laughed. "Rookie mistake."

Claudia smacked her wrists together. She was really enjoying this.

"Now spin off the top," June said.

"Like this?" Claudia asked. She turned the top of the bottle until it came off. She held the open bottle in one hand and the top with the dangling pump in the other.

"Just like that," June said. Then she reached over. "I'll

just borrow the bottle a second and show you something."
June took her other hand off the wheel and steered with her
knees. Claudia watched with great interest. "I shouldn't be
doing this, but what the heck. This is a driving trick you'll
get used to when you're doing your makeup in the crappy
sun visor mirror or flossing on your way to work." June put
her forefinger on the top of the bottle, turned it over, and set
it right again. She reached over with her perfume-dampened
finger and rubbed a couple quick circles behind Claudia's
ears. "And there you go, curly girly. That's the secret spot."

June handed the bottle back to Claudia. Claudia spun
on the top and ran her fingers around the embossed edges of
the logo on the glass. She didn't say anything. She just kept
tracing the logo. Trucks was intently listening and watching.
Was he this engaging with Claudia? He really appreciated
how June connected with her. How their energies ran together.

"Will the other kids like me if I wear this?" Claudia
asked, without looking away from the bottle.

June looked at Claudia. She reached over and ran her
hand through Claudia's hair. "You sweet thing," she said.

"I'm afraid," Claudia said.

"Of what?" June asked.

"The kids in Nevada. That they'll make fun of my hearing phones."

Hearing aids. Trucks thought it but said nothing.

"Oh, darling," June said. "You cherub thing."

Claudia grabbed June's hand and held it to her cheek.
Closed her eyes. Sighed like it's all she ever wanted.

Trucks watched the closeness they were sharing. He felt

a pain inside. Something so deep he didn't even know. He ached with a fear that had bled through him since he lost his girl the last time. And he'd decided it would be the truly last time. No matter what. And he'd do all he could to protect her waning innocence from hardship or struggle or pain or loss. Despite this beautiful moment, everything in his being said this: *Go. Go.* They must always go.

THE GRAY KARMA

They stood outside the Archibald Suites. It was cold and dark. Winter's dusk always comes early. Claudia pouted away from Trucks with her arms folded over her chest. She wouldn't look at him.

Trucks had turned down June's offer to take showers in her hotel room and rest. Now he had his thumb out, trying to pick up rides from the parking lot exit back onto the interstate. He'd tied the Hallowell sack to one of the belt loops on the side of his pants so he wouldn't have to hold it. There were cans of beans in there and the toothpaste, the brushes, the skinny metal can opener, some bottles of water, a jar of peanut butter, and rice cakes.

Trucks turned away from the road and looked at Claudia. "Are you done pouting?"

"No," she said. She breathed hard. Her shoulders came up and down.

"Come help me hitch."

"She said we could have showers. It's cold. I feel icky. I wanna be warm and clean and sleep in a real bed."

"Don't you think I feel disgusting and wanna rest too? I've got dried blood on my face, swollen to high hell knuckles, and haven't slept in—forget it."

"So let's go back. She's looking at us through the window.

Pinky promise. I can see her up there."

Trucks turned, but he didn't see June in any of the windows. Most of the room lights were on. Half-drawn drapes and silhouettes of standing lamps. Nothing more.

"You don't wanna owe people," Trucks said.

"Huh?"

"First it's showers and rest. Then what? What comes after?"

"A puppy?"

Trucks laughed. "No, you knucklehead. At least look at me when we're talking. Come on."

Claudia turned toward him. "But now I can't see her in the window." Claudia looked back at the rising windows of the Archibald. Her desperation made him nervous. She put one of her big-gloved hands to her brow. She scoured the building, standing on her tiptoes. "And it's getting colder. We'll freeze."

"You don't know that."

Claudia looked at him again. "So? We still could. Come on, please?"

"I don't know," Trucks said. He looked at the passing cars, their headlights stabbing the dark. How many more would zip by?

"So what comes after? I don't get it," Claudia said.

"Nothing."

"Tell me. I wanna know."

"No."

"Tell me what comes after the showers and rest."

Deeper attachment. Connection. Disappointment. Loss. Heartbreak.

"It's complicated."

"You always say that."

"Well, everything *is* complicated."

"Can we make it *not* that way?"

"You can't undo the way the world works."

"What stuff *can* we undo?"

Trucks thought for a moment. "Just try to do everything as perfectly as possible the first go round so you don't have to have conversations about how to undo the mistakes you've made."

"Like what sorta mistakes? Are they really bad?"

"Sometimes the mistake isn't some huge thing. Sometimes you do something simple, something stupid, like fall in love."

"But that looks happy."

"Yeah, well it won't be stupid when you grow up and you do it, okay? It's only stupid for some of us. And sometimes you make a choice or take a path or tie your life to a person and it all gets fucked up beyond your wildest imagination. And then you wonder if it's because the world's just set on some path of chaos or because you built up some dark karma over time. And lots of nights you lay awake wondering if you deserve these things or not. And that can really mess with you, so don't go thinking like that."

Claudia looked confused.

"No swears," she said.

"Sorry. I'll work on it. Look, I don't know what I'm talking about, anyway. It's late, and we're both tired."

"But what's dark camera?"

"Karma."

"It sounds like candy."

"Well, it's not. Some people think you build up karma over your life. The more good you do, the more good or light karma comes your way. The more bad you do—you get the idea."

"Are we good-karma people?"

"You're a great-karma person. I know that much."

"But you?"

"I don't know. Probably grayish karma."

"What's that?"

"We all build up a good amount of both kinds of karma. You just want the light to outweigh the dark in the end. But to outweigh it all your life would be best. There's still hope for you to do that."

Claudia stood there. Thinking. Then she looked up at him. "So you tried to do good a lot, but sometimes it didn't work, and you turned gray? And then there was mistakes and Mama disappeared."

Claudia bit the fingers of her glove.

Trucks tried to think. There was a buzz in his mind. His brain still rattled from the fist-to-noggin damage a few nights before. His girl was cold, and he needed to do right by her. So he took her by the shoulders, spun her toward the Archibald Suites, and said, "Jesus Christ, Pepper Flake, is she up in the window or not?"

CATCHING THE GHOST

June hadn't been standing at any of the windows. Trucks and Claudia found her in the hotel lounge. She was sitting on a stool with her legs crossed, a cocktail in front of her. One of her white pumps dangled off her heel.

"A milk for the lady?" June said.

Claudia sat in the middle.

"We're really on a budget," Trucks said. "I've got some waters in here." He pointed to their Hallowell sack.

"I'll pay," June said. "Problem solved."

"Plus, it'll help my bones," Claudia said.

Trucks put the sack on the stool next to him.

"Can't beat that," June said. "Would you like a drink, Ezzard?"

Trucks paused. Then he remembered his false name.

"I don't drink anymore."

"We have coffee," the bartender said. He'd seemingly come out of nowhere. "Or we can do fresh-squeezed juices, smoothies, infused teas."

"What sorta tea?" Trucks asked.

"I can bring you a tea list."

"No, it's all right," Trucks said.

"We have an organic rooibos. How about that? It's imported from South Africa. It's quite high in antioxidants."

"That's a long way to go for some tea."

The bartender looked at June, then back to Trucks.

"I'll try it," Trucks said.

"Sure thing," the bartender said. "Anything else?"

Trucks noticed some cut lemons on a saucer behind the bar.

"How about some of those lemons?" Trucks pointed. "Are they extra?"

The bartender laughed. "Not at all," he said. He gave June an awkward smile and walked away.

"So you decided to wise up and come inside where it's warm," June joked.

"Apparently," Trucks said.

"It's freezing outside," Claudia said. "Feel."

Claudia put out her hands, and June held them.

"Aren't you a little icicle!" June said.

"It's not so bad. We didn't have heat sometimes," Claudia said.

"Oh," June said. She looked at Trucks.

"We lived in a rough part of town. Sometimes when the winters got real bad with heavy snow and ice, we'd lose power. The city worked on our lines last. The poor folks, you know, don't matter much to them." But it wasn't always that. Sometimes he didn't have the money to pay the utility bill or forgot to do it. Sometimes both.

June thought for a moment. She said, "A lot of snow and ice storms in Georgia?"

Claudia looked at Trucks.

"We were in Maryland for a while," he said.

June nodded. She rubbed Claudia's hands real fast to

warm them up. She made whooshing sounds when she did it. They smiled at each other. Like two glowing orbs.

Trucks looked at the bartender. He opened an orange tin and used a metal tea-leaf infuser to scoop out the tea. He dipped the infuser in purified water, hooked it on the edge of a fancy teacup with purple flowers painted on it, and poured in boiling water. He capped the teacup and let it sit. Claudia's milk sat on the back bar with a straw in it.

"What's yours?" Claudia asked June.

"It's a Jack Rose."

"I like it all pink. It looks pretty."

"People don't drink these old-time cocktails anymore," June said. She picked up her glass and took a sip.

"How come?" Claudia asked.

"Some things just go out of style. Though, believe it or not, I live on Jack Rose Court. Imagine that. Of all the names." She looked at Trucks.

The bartender set Claudia's milk in front of her.

"I can make yours pink too," the bartender said.

"Yes!" Claudia said.

The bartender held up a finger, gave her a wink, and walked away. Trucks didn't like that the bartender could hear everything so well. The guy seemed nosey.

The bartender came back with a bottle of strawberry syrup and a small plate. He squeezed a few drops of syrup into the pale milk. Soon it was pink, and Claudia was happy. She swirled the milk with her straw. The bartender set down the small plate; it had two cherries on it. He slid the plate between Claudia and June, and they gave each other a big-eyed, open-mouthed look.

"Well, thanks a million," June said.

"A bajillion," Claudia said.

"My pleasure," the bartender said. He checked on the tea, then said to Trucks, "I'll let it steep a few more minutes." He gave Trucks the saucer of cut lemons and walked to the end of the bar.

Claudia sipped her now-pink milk. She watched it go through the straw. Then she blew bubbles. June took a drink. Trucks looked down at his hands.

Out of nowhere, Trucks said, "I fought a guy named Jack Rose once. But he went by Holly. Everyone called him Holly Houdini because you couldn't hit the guy. Like he was there one second, you'd step in to throw a short punch, and he'd weave under it or bob out and come off the center line and smack you in the head. In. Out. It was magic, really. It was." Trucks looked at his tea, still sitting behind the bar. Steam rose in curls off its rim.

"What happened to him?" June asked.

"He went to train in Detroit. Won titles in three weight classes. He's probably considered a legend by now. I only fought him that once."

"Did you win?" Claudia asked.

Trucks laughed. "Not a chance, Pepper Flake. Not a fucking chance."

June laughed.

"The swears," Claudia said.

Trucks nodded. Then he said, "I surprised him with a huge left. It was the eighth round, and I could tell he was loading up on his right and hoping to take me out with it. He had all his weight on his back foot and his shoulder slightly dipped. It's the kinda stuff you learn to watch for. Anyway, I feinted to my left, and sure enough he threw a hard overhand right. I weaved under and popped him with a power left hook to the temple. I couldn't have thrown it any harder. It was the most devastating punch I ever threw. Holly stumbled back, but the ropes caught him. Held him up like that with his arms stretched out. It was like catching a ghost. The crowd was stunned. Hell, even I was stunned, and it took me a second to snap out of it. I saw that blood waving down his cheek. That bright red kinda brought me back to life, you know, like a bull. It put a real charge in me. He staggered off the ropes, and I went after him throwing crazy combinations that missed, one after the other. Damn, he was elusive. And I was exhausted as hell by then and didn't catch him again after that. Not even once. Not even barely. I'm not sure too many boxers ever did touch him."

"That's a wild story," June said. She pinched the stem of her glass.

"That damn ghost," Trucks said. He shook his aching head.

Claudia had been fixed on him the whole time. Trying to take in his story. Make sense of it. She looked forward and sipped on her straw.

"Sorry about that," the bartender said. He'd come back over from the end of the bar. "Here's your tea, just the right temperature. Would you like anything else?"

"That'll do," Trucks said.

"For the ladies?"

"That'll do," Claudia said.

Trucks worked the kinks out of his left hand. Then he

grabbed lemon after lemon, squeezing the juice into his tea. Some of the seeds came with it. No big deal. The bartender probably hated how he was ruining this first-class South African tea. Trucks didn't care. A trainer had told him lemons were good for cleaning the liver. He trusted that. Trucks took a long sip of tea, now sour. The bartender walked off.

"How about we eat these cherries?" June said. She handed one to Claudia and took one for herself. "None for you, big guy," June said to Trucks. "Must be ladies' night."

"Sure looks like it," Trucks said.

June pinched the stem and held up her cherry to Claudia. "To new friends," she said.

"To new friends," Claudia said.

They bumped the little red buds against one another and ate the cherries. Then they set the dark stems on the plate.

"Well, no shit," Trucks said, really to himself.

"What's that?" June said.

"Just thinking out loud."

"The swears," Claudia said.

"Sorry," Trucks said.

"At least your bruiseity brains are working," Claudia said. Trucks tapped his head.

June asked for the bill and paid with cash. Trucks gulped the rest of his tea. Then he grabbed the Hallowell sack and stood.

"Now, how about those hot showers?" June said, closing her pocketbook.

"I get to go first!" Claudia said.

"And you?" June asked Trucks.

"That's such a nice offer with the showers, but we really

don't wanna trouble you. And you gave us a ride and bought our drinks. It's plenty, really."

"It's no trouble. I'd welcome it."

Claudia tugged on Trucks's coat.

"All right. Let's have her take one first, then we'll see," he said.

Claudia ran over and hugged June. June's cheeks turned red from either the surprise of the hug or some kind of deep affection.

"Come on, then, curly girly," June said, and took Claudia's hand.

The three of them walked out of the lounge. Trucks felt the swift ache in his temple. After a few strides into the lobby he looked back at the bartender wiping down the bar top where they'd been. Trucks saw the dark cherry stems on the small plate. He thought about the last time he'd had a drink. He thought about protecting his girl. He thought about the ghost of Holly Jack Rose and wondered what the hell cherries had to do with anything.

THE REAL GOOD

Claudia sang in the bath. She didn't want a shower once she saw the jacuzzi tub with the pressure jets.

"Don't forget to wash your personals, Pepper Flake," Trucks said through the door. Then he realized she couldn't hear him without her hearing aids. He listened to her singing for a moment before walking away.

"She's wonderful, you know," June said, when he came into the room.

"Sometimes I really don't know how she turned out like this, but I thank my lucky punches. I really do."

June sat on a love seat in the middle of the room. It faced the king-size bed. Trucks walked over to the window and pulled the curtain aside. Saw harsh parking lot lights. The darkened interstate in the distance. No noise. That expensive, super-thick glass that keeps it all out. So dense. Like it could stop bullets.

"I know you said you don't drink anymore, but can I get you something from the fridge? I helped myself to a beer. I craved that cocktail after the long drive, but I'm really more of a beer girl."

Trucks looked from the window to June. She held a green bottle of imported beer. She took a drink. He fixated on how her lips wrapped around the spout. How long had it been?

Jesus, how long?

"Thanks, but we have some waters still." Trucks pointed to their sack of supplies. He'd hung it on a desk chair. Their coats were draped over the backrest. Their boots near the door. Always ready.

"You can help yourself, if you want," June said. "That's all I'm saying."

Trucks watched the blinking taillights of cars on the distant interstate. Like red stars moving at hyper speeds across an asphalt universe.

"You can come over here and hang out," June said. "I'd like to hear more about your trip."

Trucks rubbed the curtain between his fingers. Then he let go, walked over, and sat on the end of the bed. He faced June sitting on the love seat.

"Tell me about you," Trucks said. "About your life in Sioux Falls. You've heard enough about us. I don't really wanna think about our life right now."

June looked up at the ceiling as if there was so much weight to his question. Then she leaned forward and put her elbows on her knees. She held the beer with both hands and spun the bottle. Then she looked up at Trucks.

"You really want to know," she said.

"Sure," he said.

"I didn't mean it as a question. I can see it in your face."

Trucks reached up and touched around his bad eye. Felt the rough, dried blood. The seams.

June took a hand off the bottle. She reached out to Trucks. He reached back, reflexive, and took hold of her hand. They held hands for a moment. Hers so soft and warm. His cold and rough. He traced the veins on the top of her hand with his thumb. Then he let go.

"Whoa," June said, sounding breathless. Her eyes were big and bright.

Trucks nodded. Then he stood and walked over to the bathroom door. He listened in on his girl. His body pulsed. He opened and closed his left hand, made a fist, ran his knuckles along the soft grain of the door. Trucks could hear Claudia spinning in the jacuzzi, slapping the surface of the water. Trucks wished she had friends to play with. He listened to her song and the splashing and felt the pulse in his throat. The jacuzzi engines churning. Making that low, hard hum press against everything.

He walked back to the main room. June was sitting cross-legged on the love seat. She'd put the beer on the end table and had her hands in her lap. She scratched at an invisible blemish on her dark pants. Then she looked at him.

"Do you want to sit here?" she asked.

"Okay," he said.

He walked over and sat next to her. There was a warm static between them. Claudia's song echoed through the hotel room.

"My husband left me this year," June said. She really looked Trucks in the eye when she spoke. He wasn't used to that. "He worked for Hammer-On. He started out selling guitars in one of their shops, then worked for their custom division. He sold strings, modified scratch plates, unique pickups, fancy volume knobs and saddles and selector switches, and I listened to him go on about that job for too many hours. Anyway, he made his way up to corporate. He climbed like all those other suited robots. We started drifting when he took the desk job. He stayed out later and later with his bosses and 'the boys.' He'd come home with scratches on his neck, smelling of Tanqueray and so many random perfumes you'd think he'd stopped every half-mile home to take a shot and mess around with some other woman. He wouldn't even look at me, like I wasn't something to desire or want or remotely care about. And he even said one day after an intense argument that he didn't respect what I did, working as an art teacher, and that it wasn't really a profession and didn't bring in equal money. That *we* weren't equal. He didn't see any value in what I did and what I cared about. Well, no kidding my salary wasn't going to equal his or even come close. But I get so much joy out of helping those kids finger paint and learn how to dip and dry brushes and help them tie and untie their smocks. Every day we'd spread out their little canvases and fill the vast white spaces with splashes of color and life, all those tiny hands moving so fast and learning so much so quickly. The lights of their small spirits have always made my day and urged me forward, through even the hardest moments."

June paused. Claudia was singing. Only calm came from the window. Like there was no other sound.

"I'm totally barren," June said.

She put a hand to her mouth.

Trucks didn't move.

June cried hard.

Trucks didn't know what to do. He grabbed her wrist and held on.

June shook as she cried.

"And...and even though I told him there were other options, other avenues...he...he still left me pretty soon after that," she said.

Trucks kept holding.

June turned into him. She thrust herself into his arms and cried into his shoulder.

"There," Trucks said. "Hey. Hey."

He tried to imagine the last time a woman had confided in him.

June breathed heavy into his shoulder.

"I know I shouldn't even be telling you this, a near stranger, but there it is," she said.

"It's okay," he said. "It means something that you told me."

June pulled back and looked in his eyes.

"You're a genuine man," she said. "You don't know the kind of sweet you are."

June sat back in the love seat and wiped her eyes. She grabbed the beer from the end table and took a drink. Then she said, "So just to be clear, the nice car, the huge house on Jack Rose Court, the expensive things—they're not my lifestyle. They're not me. They're a part of who I tried to be to fit with who he'd become. Shit," June said, and laughed, "his parents even had this gaudy pewter statue of a polo horse shipped to the house. It's huge! And it's been sitting in the backyard all year. The neighbors started complaining to each other and talking behind my back about how I needed to get rid of it because it's such an eyesore to the neighborhood and might bring down their property values. But it's *his* silly eyesore of a horse, not mine, and if they want to get rid of it so badly then they can call him up and have him do something about it, or they can pay to have the damn thing hauled out of there. Like I care."

June gripped the bottle like she was trying to shatter it.

Trucks let her breathe. He let the frustration flow out of her.

Then he calmly said, "Or you could take a torch and melt it down. Turn it into a stream of lava. A hot-orange moat around the house. That'd really piss them off."

June spit out a little beer and wiped it from her chin. "And keep them out. I like the thought of that."

They looked at each other. They were at ease. It made him turn inside.

Claudia stopped singing. Trucks stood and walked toward the bathroom. June tipped the green bottle back for the last sip of beer. Midway through her swig, Trucks was back. He got on a knee, kissed his thumb, and ran it over her eyebrow. Then he traced his fingertip along her temple, down her cheek, and brushed his fingernails along her neck.

"I'm really sorry about everything," he whispered. "About being barren and that dickhead husband. I've seen the way you light up my little girl's world. I'm thankful for it. And you're right, there are other avenues. And you'll seek them and have them. This shit never should have happened to you, any of it. And all I can offer is the bond of knowing what it's like to be left, and you never deserved that. I know you know what you are. You know your worth. I can see it. You're not broken by this. You won't ever be. I've got so many breaks inside me, I wouldn't ever want you to see them." Trucks looked at the floor. "I wouldn't want anyone to see."

Trucks looked up at June. "Some things are unmendable. But you. You've got all this buried potential left. It's deep down in there, and you'll keep reaching. You'll find it. And you'll see all that good inside you. The real good."

Claudia called out again from the bathroom. He could hear her splashing.

"That's what I've got left," he said. "That's all my good right there, waiting for me in the other room."

PERSPECTIVE

Nighttime over Kadoka. Population: 690. All quiet.

The strips of interstate were clear.

The Archibald Suites parking lot was lit in a casted white from hovering streetlamps.

Up three floors.

June turned off the light. She clicked on a small lamp that gave a negligible glow. She stared out the window into the winter night. Unbuttoned her blouse. Took off her itchy bra. She slid her tight pants down. Kept her panties on. Put on wool socks. June looked at her reflection in the window. Pushed her breasts together. Let them drop. She grabbed her hips and squeezed. Dug her nails in before putting on a big nightshirt. She laid down on the too-big bed. Took the far edge of it. Away from the window.

Across the room.

The door slightly ajar. The bathroom steamed up. Claudia had already pulled her pajamas from the radiator and put them on. Trucks took strands of her hair and gently dried them on a towel. Then tugged on the pink cuffs of her pajamas, still snug around her ankles. Wiggled her toes between his fingers. Stuck out his tongue. Trucks put the toilet cover down and sat Claudia on the seat. Brushed her hair with his fingers. Cleaned her ears with complimentary swabs from a small dish. Used his wipes to sanitize her hearing aids, then gently hooked one to each ear. Tested the volume. Lightly pressed her cheeks. Held her by the shoulders. Face to face. And told her what had to be done.

THE PRETENSE OF SLEEP

They'd all lain down together. June on the side of the bed near the door, Trucks on the side near the window, Claudia in the middle. And it was nice like that for a while. A kind of peace to the beats of their near bodies at rest.

Hours had passed. June was out from the drinks. Trucks put on his workman's coat. He got down on his knees and helped Claudia into her coat and the oversized gloves as quietly as possible. The zipping and snapping could wait. Their sack of supplies was out in the hallway. The hotel room door cracked open.

"It's time," Trucks whispered.

Claudia was crying.

Trucks moved to get up. Claudia grabbed his arm.

"Why?" she said.

Trucks put a finger to his lips. He gave her a stern look. They were at the end of the bed.

"But why?" she whispered.

June rolled in her sleep. She spoke gibberish. Trucks put his hand over Claudia's mouth. They stayed like that for a while. A streak of moonlight coming through the window.

June let out a long breath, clearly lost in a dream.

Trucks took his hand from Claudia's mouth. They looked in each other's eyes. He wiped Claudia's tears with his thumbs. She pushed his hands away. Trucks felt sick. But he'd be sick no matter what they did, and this is what he'd chosen. He knew no other way.

Trucks put a finger to his lips again. He stood and nodded toward the door. Claudia looked away. Trucks put a hand on her shoulder. Then Claudia reached out and squeezed June's foot. He allowed her this.

Seconds went by. Seconds like minutes to a man always going.

Soon Claudia relented. She had to. She let go and walked with Trucks out into the harsh yellow light of the hallway. Trucks gently closed the door. He pulled a note from his pocket, like a lead weight in his hand, and slipped it under the door. With his back turned, Claudia ran down the long hall, tearing across the burgundy carpet. Its navy diamond pattern flashing between footfalls. She slammed through the exit door. Ran down the stairwell.

Something about her ferocious running made Trucks feel a spark of pride. He followed fast, the Hallowell sack swinging from his wrist.

He caught her in the parking lot and turned her around. Dropped the sack. Pulled her into his body. They embraced under the lights of the parking lot. Their gray breaths rolling out in the cold.

Trucks stepped back. They were slightly huffing from the run. The wind whipped their faces. Cried out. Called to them. They had to keep moving.

Trucks got down on a knee and zipped Claudia's coat. Then he pulled on her hood and buttoned her throat flaps. He picked up the sack, stood, and tied it through his belt-loop. Then he scooped Claudia off the ground. She made no attempt to resist. So Trucks secured her in his arms and trudged toward the interstate through the snow-packed night. Each step a shockwave. Each movement putting him further from one fear and closer to another.

He couldn't hear Claudia's cries over the warm thrum in his head. But he could feel the vibrations of her sadness. His heart beating into his throat, that metallic taste he knew too well. Claudia dug into his arm. His girl releasing that deep anger of loss she'd come to know too well. He felt her looking back over his shoulder with each footfall, imagined her eyes darting, desperately watching the iced-over hotel windows for any sign of movement, for any bit of life.

THE BADLANDS REALITY

He carried his girl down the shoulder of I-90. The slaps of wind meant little. Hadn't he felt worse, taking so much fist-to-bone punishment all his life? He had. Of course. He had.

Whenever he heard the soft thunder of an engine, he'd stick out his thumb but resist looking back. They'd stop for him and his girl. Or they wouldn't. His beaten, ugly face would change nothing. This late in the night, his girl on his shoulder might mean nothing too. People felt anonymity in the dark. No obligation to man or pain or misfortune.

He trudged on.

West of town he could see the beginning of the Badlands. At first sight of them, he said, "Those Black Hills." But that wasn't right. They weren't there. And then he said, "You up, Pepper Flake?" His teeth were chattering. "You awake, little thing? You doing okay?"

She moved slightly. She said nothing.

A rumble. A car coming. He put out his thumb toward the road. The shine of lights grew wider on the pavement. The car zoomed on.

"You motherfucker!" he yelled. His teeth chattered hard. His head throbbed.

Trucks was thankful for his thick winter boots. For

her small white ones. And the wool socks he was sweating through. His bare hands were cold. He'd pulled his sweatshirt sleeve ends over his hands. He should have lifted some gloves from somewhere. He really hadn't thought it all out like he should have. At least Claudia was warm in his big gloves.

When he was too tired to carry her, he'd set her down, get on a knee, pull her in close. She'd mumble about being cold and tired. He'd say he knew. He wouldn't tell her he hadn't slept for days. Not even in the bed when they were all three laying in the hotel room. That he'd just stared at the ceiling at the moonlight cutting in as he listened to their sleeping breaths. Instead of talk, he'd open the throat flaps of her coat, his hands shaking, and blow out all the hot air he had in him. Right onto her cold, delicate skin. Then he'd button the coat up quick. Take off her big gloves. Rub his hands over hers as fast as possible. Blow hot air into the gloves and put them back on her. Rub her shoulders and back and legs with all the energy he had left. Anything to get his girl warm. To keep them moving.

He didn't know how far they'd gone. Several cars had passed. Claudia hung off his shoulder, tired of clinging on. Her weight immense after so much walking in the elements. The dead of night. All the cold it brings.

Trucks was exhausted. He'd trained for years. Hard physical and mental endurance the likes of which most men would never experience. All that breaking and blood loss and the sting of splitting skin. But he was older now, and he ached through all the parts of himself. Even his spirit was hurting with the cost of disappointing his girl and leaving yet another person behind.

Trucks fell to a knee and nearly dropped Claudia. He didn't hear her make a sound. But he got back up and kept walking.

His thoughts came and went like sharp echoes. Berating him for taking his girl away from the warmth. The hotel. The children's home. Had she been better off without him? No. No. He could barely think of it. It was together or it was nothing. He'd promised her this. The bitter cold could not outlast him.

"We're near the Badlands," he said to break the thoughts. "That's what they call them. I can see them out there in the distance."

He looked at Claudia on his shoulder. Pulled back her hood a little. She was out. Eyes shut tight. Mouth hanging open.

Trucks pulled her hood forward and turned to look back down the interstate. He didn't see any lights. He expected there weren't any for miles. He turned back. Walked on. Watched his breath go out. And out. And out. He felt the ache in his knees. His shoulders. His lower back.

"I'll tell you about them sometime. The big ridges."

Trucks stumbled but kept his footing.

"Way back out there. Way back. They're—"

He stumbled again. Feeling dizzy.

"They have. Out there. The hills."

He stopped. Such a rush to his head. His girl cold and limp in his arms. Starlight against the deep black, bursting galaxies in his eyes.

THE AGREEMENT

Trucks woke in the backseat of a large pickup. Claudia was tucked under his arm, sleeping against him, her back to his chest. They were wrapped in heavy wool blankets and sweating. It was bright out.

Trucks leaned on his elbow and raised up. He looked at the driver in the rearview. The driver fixed his eyes on him.

"It good to be back among the living?" the driver asked.

Trucks was groggy. He didn't know what to say.

"You crazy son-of-a-bitch," the driver whispered. He darted his eyes between Trucks and the road. "I was praying you two wouldn't be goners."

"What happened?"

"You don't remember talking to me?"

"Where are we?"

"You two were passed out beside the road. Christ, you're lucky you didn't freeze to death. Or somebody didn't roll over you, just laying there like cold carcasses."

"I remember carrying her through the snow. Looking at the big hills." Trucks breathed deep. His head was killing him. He was hot and exhausted. Claudia was still breathing heavy beside him.

"Gerald," the man said. "But you probably don't remember my name."

"I don't. I'm sorry. My head's pounding."

"You're lucky I keep a water jug and blankets in my pick-up all winter, otherwise I'd have taken you to the hospital like I wanted. You kept hollering when I told you I was gonna take you there to get the two of you checked out."

"I did?" Trucks looked down at Claudia. She breathed deep. Her eyes shut. The lids fluttering.

"You kept saying they'd take your daughter away. You scooped her outta the seat and stumbled down the middle of the interstate, you crazy bastard."

Trucks shook his head. He reached behind Claudia's uncovered ear and clicked off the hearing aid.

"So what's your real name?" Gerald asked.

"What'd I say it was?"

"Lenny. Then Alexander. Then some weird one. Buzzard or something. Heck if I can remember. What a wild night."

"Our things. What about our things?"

Gerald pointed to the passenger seat. "I scraped together as much as I could find. Most of it spilled outta the bag, I assume when you passed out. The rice cakes are smashed or left out on the tundra. The crows are having a nice breakfast. I found a couple waters. Jar of peanut butter. Soap. Stuff like that. I don't remember. And there wasn't a wallet or any money in there. So don't try to claim I robbed you. There was nothing in that torn-up bag but food and sundries. And you'll need to get new toothbrushes. Those are done for."

"Thank you. Really," Trucks said.

"I wonder if I should have just taken you to the hospital, but you didn't seem to have hypothermia, and you got so damn edgy and desperate when I suggested it. Kept yelling about how they'd take her. What'd you do? You a criminal?"

Trucks shook his head.

"Well? What then?"

"I'm not a criminal. It's just a custody issue. Nothing more than that. I'm behind on a few payments, but I'm gonna make good. I just need some time."

"Well, okay," Gerald said. "It's not my business. Thank goodness I found you when I did. Wonder how long you were laying out there."

"I don't wanna know," Trucks said. He looked down at his girl.

"So what do I call you? And here." Gerald handed Trucks a wax cup of water from his cupholder.

"Ezzard," Trucks said.

"Buzzard, Blizzard, Ezzard. I was close."

"You were."

Trucks drank the water. He thought he'd just sip it, but he couldn't control himself. He chugged it all. He gave Gerald the wax cup and asked for more. After his second cup, Trucks asked, "Where are we headed?"

"Crow Agency. Nearly there, actually. I was hoping you'd wake before we got there. Boy, this would have been a hell · of a story to tell my wife if she was still around." Gerald swallowed hard.

"Oh."

"She never did like me picking up hitchers, but I guess you two wouldn't really count."

"I guess not."

Something had shifted in Gerald's voice. Trucks tried to look out the windows. The morning light was bright and harsh. He saw everything in hazy pinks. Like he'd just come in from the snow.

"So we're nearing the state line?" Trucks asked.

"Which one?"

"South Dakota."

Gerald laughed.

"What?"

"Already crossed two state lines."

"Shit."

"Sure did."

"Which ones?"

"Went into Wyoming and up through Montana now. Like I said, nearing Crow Agency."

Trucks looked around like it would accomplish anything. Claudia didn't move.

Trucks rubbed Claudia's back. She was still out. He leaned down and whispered to her anyway. "Keep sleeping, Pepper Flake. Get all the rest you can."

"You said you were heading west," Gerald said.

Trucks looked up. "Yeah, Nevada."

Gerald smiled and slapped the wheel. "Oh boy. You didn't say anything about Nevada. Must have been that ice brain you had going on."

"This really isn't good."

"Hey, nothing wrong with Montana. You're looking to get a new start with your daughter, right?"

"That's the idea."

Gerald turned his head around to look Trucks in the eye.

"Then if you're doing what's right for her, what's in her best interest, I'm telling you, Montana's a great place to be." He turned back to watch the road. "Fresh air. Trails. Farms.

Fishing. Rivers. Family outings. Barbecues. Ranches. Shooting ranges. Cattle. That big old sky you always read about in
the outdoor magazines."

Trucks let it all sink in.

"You said you were changing your life. You told me last
night. You said you were heading toward better. And if I can
be frank here, you sure as heck didn't seem to know where
the hell better was or how to get there."

"I guess I deserve that."

"Look, you're in Montana already. Maybe twenty minutes to go until we reach my acreage. I'd be all right with
you and your daughter staying a few nights. I'm sixty-eight,
Mr. Ezzard. I'm not young. I'm not all that old, either. But
that sure as shit wasn't something smart, whatever you were
doing out there. And you're the adult. You're the man. You're
the father. It's your fault as high as fault rises. Maybe this
is all you can offer her. Maybe this is the best you can do.
But being dead doesn't do none of you any good. I can offer
warmth, some meals, open land for your daughter to play
in, and maybe some coffee and a view and some log-splitting
repayment for saving your hide. I mean no offense. Know
that. I'd like to see you both be well and good, and I'm not
sure I can just drop you off somewhere and call myself a
good man for taking you west a few hours. So that's the deal.
Take it or don't. That's what I can offer."

Gerald turned and stuck his open hand between the seats.

Trucks paused. Still delirious. Still trying to comprehend.
The night, the day, his pounding head, his girl quiet beside
him.

"Jesus, son, shake it or shit on it, I've got a road to watch."

WHAT YOU DO IN THE SUN ROOM

They were in the sun room. Gerald brought Trucks a glass of water and sat beside him at the little oak table. He had a coffee on the table. Trucks took a drink of the cold water. It hurt his throat. The two of them looked out the big windows at the frozen-over acreage. The hills banked. The crisscrossed wooden fences carried a thin layer of snow. The horse barn was empty and hollow and dark. Its doors, for whatever reason, open to the elements.

"I should check on her again," Trucks said.

"She's doing fine. Relax," Gerald said. He blew on his coffee. "Keep that blanket wrapped around you and take your time warming up. Your daughter's got a fever. It's not hypothermia, at least. What'd you expect dragging her out in the snow in these conditions? Wearing pajamas, of all things. But she'll be all right. She's young. Kids are resilient."

Trucks thought of Claudia tucked in the bed. The quilt to her chin. Her curly hair dark and wet against the bedsheets.

"I know I fucked up, all right? You don't have to keep reminding me."

Gerald took a sip. "Well," he said. Then he didn't say anything else.

"Well, what?"

"You're right. I've made enough of it. It's not something

I'll bring up again. She looks a bit like one of my grand-daughters, that's all. They might be resilient, but they're still delicate. People are only thick as skin. It don't last. That innocence dies quick. I imagine if you've been living like this a while, she hasn't got any left. Or much."

"She's got some."

"I suppose she probably does."

"She does."

"You're probably right."

Gerald took another sip. Trucks finished his water and stared out the window at the frozen hills.

Gerald said, "I'm just sharper about things now. Coarser. It's what happens when you get older. You see all the mistakes you made and fences you didn't mend. All you wanna do is protect things. No more harm or hurt or wrongdoing. It's what you strive for. The younger you are, the busier you are. It's the busy that keeps you from thinking. Keeps you from worrying so much about what the world wants. When you're young it's all about what you want. What you desire. What you don't have time for."

Trucks opened and closed his left hand under the table.

"My wife, Maddie, used to say I needed to learn to stop ranting at people."

"I deserve it," Trucks said.

"It's not about deserve. This isn't about judgment and punishment. There's just a sick girl in there, and we're working out the problems of the world in here. It's what you do in the sun room. It's what I built it for. Look around. Couple chairs, the table, some plants and flower pots. When it's too damn cold to go out there in the fields, you wait in here behind the glass. Not so different. Except you can't hear the wind the way I like. It feels artificial, you know, behind that glass. But it's got its uses."

"Protects," Trucks said.

"The main use."

"Sure."

"You know a lot about it."

"I think so."

"Good."

Gerald held his coffee against his big belly. He felt his beard with his free hand. Twisted a grip of scruff.

"So what's your trade?" Gerald asked.

"Boxing."

"Ah. What's your weight class?"

"Welter to light-heavy. I move around a lot."

"You can pick up more action that way."

"You sound like you know."

"I boxed through my teens," Gerald said. He leaned forward, set his coffee down, and showed Trucks his knuckles. Shaved down, crooked. His right hand swollen on the outside where a punch had landed wrong and the break never set right. Trucks could read his knuckles like a rough map.

"How'd you do?" Trucks asked.

"I did all right. No record to brag about. Got my bell rung a lot, but that's no unique story. I grew up out in Moscow, Idaho. You ever been?"

Trucks shook his head.

"For a while we had some youth violence problems. Some real troublemakers. I was part of the problem. Around that time some progressive contemplative nuns moved into our college town and turned the old roller rink into a commune for the Sisters of St. Agnes of Latah County. They set out to solve the youth problem by starting a boxing club, of all things."

"No shit," Trucks said.

"I boxed in that club for years. It helped a lot of us rural kids with too much time and pent-up aggression. If we were gonna be violent or destructive, might as well learn to harness it and release that energy in a controlled space with a new skill. Not out there on the streets making life worse for everyone."

Gerald grabbed his coffee and took a sip. Trucks slid his glass over the oak table, back and forth between his hands.

"You think the boxing helped you?" Gerald asked. "Like some kind of saving grace?"

Trucks leaned back in the chair. He folded his arms and thought about it. Had the boxing saved him? Or was it just about the movement in the ring? Could it have been anything that combined skill, grace, concentration, precision, and raw power? Had it chosen him? Had he chosen it? Or was it about something else? Punishment, maybe.

"I wouldn't call it that," Trucks said. "What did it save me from? Where did it lead me? I don't know. This is the only life I've had. It's all I know and all I understand. If I could go back and look at the other paths, see where they went, then I'd know if it saved me somehow from a worse life. But maybe it stopped me from finding something better too. You can't really know with these kinds of things." Trucks paused. "But look, I'm not going down that road. It's too long and dark and full of regrets and could haves and things that don't make your mind right. I've spent so many years hustling just to get to this place, and it's okay enough. And maybe I can come clean for my girl and quit the boxing. Think of it like an oath. I don't know. It's been rattling around in there for a while. Like maybe I could take up other things. Like I could figure it out. But the only thing I know for sure is as long as I'm doing okay and I've got my girl, then everything's right with the world and whatever I'm capable of being or doing."

Trucks stared out the window. The whole time he'd expected to see movement. An arc of flying birds. But it was still out there. Cold and still and heavy white.

"I get you," Gerald said. "Where you're coming from. I've not been to your places, but your cloth isn't cut so far from mine. Don't fool yourself about that. And you talk a lot about your daughter. It's clear how much you care for her. How much you've sacrificed. I can see that. Any idiot could see that in your eyes."

Trucks shook off the blanket, stood, and walked to the windows. His back to Gerald.

"Not trying to offend," Gerald said.

"It's all right," Trucks said.

"I wanted to ask about the mother. You don't say any—"

"The ride here. You'd said something about splitting wood. You got wood to split?"

"Well, sure. I've got wood to split, but you should really rest. You two were so zonked out on that highway. Cold as clams. I think you should get that blanket back on and sleep."

"I'd like to do some of that work. I owe you. Let me work it off."

"Well."

"I know my body. It'll hold. Where do you keep your axes?"

"In the shed near the horse barn, but—"

"What kind of axes do you keep?"

"Splitting mauls, felling axes, Hudson Bays."

"You got a go-devil?"

"Last time I checked."

"Good."

"You sure?"

"I'll sweat it out. It'll be okay."

Gerald swished his coffee. "Okay's pretty damn relative," he said.

SHADOWBOXING THROUGH THE
RADIANT WHITE

Trucks took measure on the next log. Axe out. Arms
steady. Feeling the grip of the handle. Then he lifted the axe
overhead. Brought it down in a swift movement.

Thunk.

Split another clean piece off. Then he sliced the halves
into quarters.

He'd been at it over an hour and went through nearly all
the unsplit wood. Not because he had the energy—he was
exhausted—but because he had so much intensity to release.

Trucks set another log on the chopping block. His muscles were sore. He felt the ache of that old left hand he'd
thrown so many times. The sting of it felt good in a way. He
was so used to clenching his hands inside his boxing gloves
that grasping the handle felt like a piece of home he'd left
behind.

He set the axe on the log. Took measure. Focused. Raised.

Thunk. Thunk. Thunk.

Trucks was sweaty from all the work. Winter or not, he
took off his workman's coat and tossed it on the woodpile. It
was covered by a dark tarp to keep off the snow except where
Trucks had peeled it back to stack the cut wood. He leaned
the go-devil against the chopping block and picked the split

pieces from the ground, then added them to the woodpile.

Trucks grabbed his collar and shook out his shirt. Then he walked away from the pile, out into the open snow. A soft orange glow came from behind the gray clouds. The arches of the hills reached up to the big sky.

The movement called to him. He ached without it.

Trucks threw a jab with his left, bobbed under a phantom right cross, and followed with a hook.

Pah-pah.

He circled. Stepped with grace on his toes. His footwork and movement feeling foreign in the heavy winter boots and unfamiliar snow.

Another incoming straight. Trucks slipped, weaved under. Slid out of range.

Trucks stepped in. Threw a combination—jab-cross-hook.

Pah-pah-pah.

He watched his breath float between punches, then slipped out again.

Found his distance.

Threw the jumping lead hook.

Pah.

And back out again. Trucks circled. Feinted in. Popped out.

Pah. Pah-pah-pah.

Trucks rolled his shoulder. Dodged a cross. Bobbed. Weaved. Bobbed. Circled out.

He thought about his girl sweating under that thick quilt.

His boots went whoosh-whoosh in the snow.

Countered with an uppercut. Followed with a double

jab.

Pah. Pah-pah.

Kept that motherfucker off.

Another barrage incoming. Trucks used his footwork. Head movement. Reminded himself that he didn't fear tired.

His girl was sleeping. She didn't feel well. But she'd be well again soon. They'd be back.

He threw that classic one-two. Jab to right cross.

Pah-pah.

Got his distance. Breath coming out like hot smoke. Measured. Feet churning. He was making pictures in the snow.

Rolled the shoulder. Head under. Parried. Parried. Wove. Spun out.

Jab. Jab. Straight. Jab. Flurry.

Pah-pah. Pah. Pah. Pah-pah-pah-pah.

And now he was losing breath. Was it the altitude? All that chopping? It was hard to keep his hands up. His chin tucked. He knew he was fading.

Pah-pah.

He had to keep going.

Slipped. Rolled. Got out.

Pah. Pah-pah. Pah.

He was alive, hearing his breath like that. The blood in his throat. The shake of his shoulders. His fists balled and striking. The grit of his nails digging into his palms.

Circled. Circled. Pushed away. Kept out of the clinch.

Pah. Pah.

Sidestepped.

Pah.

He was cramping up. His head hot. The sweat rolling off him in the bitter morning. His body going on instinct, his mind working only in images.

He'd go inside and see her soon. But now. Now was his. A few more punches.

Pah-pah. Pah.

Parried. Parried. Lean-in uppercut.

Pah.

A few more movements.

Pah-pah.

Trucks walked the phantom down with a darting reach.

Pah-pah-pah.

Lighting him up. Furious punches. A blur of fists and spit. To the head. The body. Head. Body. Left. Right. Bam. Bam. Bam.

The people in the bingo hall would cheer with such a wall-thumping echo. He could hear it in a haze. They'd call out. They'd say his name. His girl would be there. She'd be big-eyed smiling and clapping. He could really see her there with the heavy ring lights above. All the radiant white. And he could see this and that and that and that. But all he could hear now was the whir of the blazing wind. The whoosh of his boots. The hisses of gray breath as his punches rolled out.

Pah-pah. Pah-pah-pah-pah.

She'd see him bleeding in that ring years down the road. His hand raised. Understand what he'd given his life to. Know that he mattered out in that gritty world in some way. That he'd made something for them and done good by her. And maybe it would happen then. On that day when she saw him bleeding in the ring a winner. When she looked up at his busted face through the coiled ropes. Thinking *father*. Thinking *proud*. Maybe it didn't have to be something he imagined. Maybe it could really happen like that.

THE WAITING

Trucks wore some of Gerald's clothes as he sat in a chair beside the guest bed, watching over Claudia. He didn't feel like himself in the corduroy pants and black-and-red-checkered flannel. But Gerald had offered to throw their clothes in the wash, and Trucks couldn't say no. They hadn't cleaned or changed their clothes in days.

Gerald appeared in the doorway.

Trucks looked up.

"I think she'll be out for a while," Gerald said. "Why don't you come have some supper?"

"How long, do you think? How long will she be like this?"

"Through the night, I'd guess."

Trucks looked back to Claudia.

"I've seen worse," Gerald said. "So much worse. Trust that your little one's going to be glowing again soon."

Gerald's words didn't soothe Trucks. He looked over his girl, pulled tight into the covers. Her head was off to one side. Her cheeks pale.

Trucks waited for Gerald to leave the room.

Then he put his forehead on the bed and cried into the sheets.

DINNER WITHOUT HER

Trucks hadn't eaten meat in a while. With trying to pay off all his debts to get Claudia back, he couldn't afford it. He'd subsisted off sweet potatoes and black beans for so long. Now he had a tender cut of elk in front of him, and it didn't feel satisfying.

"How many pieces you gonna cut that into before you take a bite?" Gerald asked.

"Not trying to be rude," Trucks said. "I just can't get this off my mind."

"We need to get you thinking about something else. You want some more tea?"

Gerald stood and took the pitcher of tea from the counter. He brought it over and refilled Trucks's glass.

"At least you're keeping hydrated," Gerald said.

Trucks spun the glass a few times. Looked at the faded flower patterns. He felt the etchings with his fingertips. Traced them. "These are nice," he said. "The glasses."

"They were handed down in my wife's family. They're a lot older than you'd think. I used to just let them sit up in the cupboards, fearing one of the grandkids would drop them when visiting. But I figured, why the hell have them if you're not gonna use them, right? Besides, Maddie always loved using the glasses and the matching plates. It reminded her of her parents, her grandparents. All those old people she was used to. Now it brings me memories of her. The more I can touch things she touched…shit, I don't know."

"It's a nice thing," Trucks said.

Gerald cut a piece of elk and ate it. He chewed and looked out the window. He was wearing flannel too.

"Can I ask where she is?" Trucks said.

"My wife?"

"Yeah."

"Out in the flower fields over the ridge. You can see them just beyond where you were splitting that wood to-day. Though no flowers are growing now, obviously. Come spring they're impossible to miss."

"Must be something," Trucks said.

"Hey, thanks again for your labor. I do appreciate it. You handled that axe with class." Gerald took another bite. He kept his elbow on the table, the fork lifted.

"Buried?" Trucks asked.

"What's that?"

"She's buried out there?"

"Sprinkled, more like it. She wanted to be cremated and have the ashes taken where it suited me best. So I put her out with all the beautiful flowers, where she belongs. The whole of her scattered among colorful petals and white roots. There's something nice about that. Honorable." Gerald looked out the window again. "God dammit, I loved her so much."

Trucks looked over Gerald's face. His lip quivering. A sadness in his eyes, like the memory was heavy on him. Trucks picked up his glass and took a drink. He thought about his girl in bed, how just before dinner he'd held her wrist and felt the blinking pulse, just to be sure.

"Can I ask how you lost her?" Trucks said.

Gerald laughed. "What a funny way to put it."

"I didn't mean anything by it."

Gerald set his fork down. Put his hands behind his head, his fingers interlocked. He leaned back in his chair, closed his eyes.

"Asphyxiation," Gerald said.

"Oh," Trucks said.

"She had this rare disorder called Cyclic Vomiting Syndrome. Not many people have it. It came and went, but when it came, it came hard. She'd throw up for hours, and her throat would get raw and red. The docs had no idea what triggered it, and when it came on, all you could do was hope it'd subside. About three years ago, I was out working the fields and came in for lunch. It was odd she hadn't called for me, and I couldn't find her on the porch or in the living room. I went into the bedroom and saw her on the floor. She'd been taking a nap in our bed, I guess, and had an episode. She threw up in her sleep and choked on the vomit. I think she probably tried to fight it and ended up on the floor. She was just lying there turning stiff, all blue and gone. An awful fucking sight. Just pure awful."

Neither of them spoke for a while. Trucks looked down at his plate. Gerald opened his eyes and sat up straight. Took a sip of tea. Then he folded his hands on the table.

"I'm really sorry," Trucks finally said.

"I appreciate it," Gerald said. He looked ahead at nothing.

"That's real devastation," Trucks said.

"We all have our versions of it," Gerald said.

"That's right," Trucks said.

Gerald looked at Trucks.

"I can tell you've known a good deal of loss," Gerald said.

"I don't wanna get into it."

Trucks opened and closed his bad hand.

"Nobody's saying you have to."

"You asked about her mama this morning, and maybe I could tell you about that. I've probably needed to tell someone."

"Sure, if it feels right. I wasn't trying to pry earlier."

Trucks looked up at the ceiling. Thick wooden beam supports crossed overhead. *Rafters.*

"She worked the corners around the bingo hall where the boxing matches were. Lots of local guys in the crowd all jacked up on adrenaline and blood and the rush of violence. There's nothing they wanted more after watching a few slugfests than to break someone's jaw or go and get off. It was easy for Elle to pick out any guy she wanted and screw him in the alley for a quick twenty. In the winter she'd come inside during the fights to get out of the cold and see if she could hook a guy. One night she caught one of my fights. Said she was so hung up on watching me in the ring that for several rounds she didn't even think about the dicks she should have been pulling. She just watched me move and work my punches. I guess she liked my vibe in the ring. That's how she put it. But I didn't meet her that night. It was a few months later after a big fight I had with Sammy Brunson out of Waukesha. The ref called the fight after only two rounds because of a deep cut I'd opened over Sammy's right eye. Think I caught him flush with a cross, then clipped him with the butt of my glove on a hook. I think he got cut open by the shit tape job on the glove more than anything. Poor kid. But anyway, it wasn't much of a fight, so some of the boys tossed a robe on me, and we went down the block to this dive called the Silver Saint. We took stools at the bar, and I popped open the robe. I still had on my trunks and knuckle tape, but nobody gave a shit. You still with me?"

"Following," Gerald said.

"So the boys ordered pitchers of Milwaukee's Best and some shots of well gin."

Gerald looked disgusted.

"What?" Trucks said.

"Might as well drink paint thinner."

"It was all we could afford, and a drink was a drink back then."

"I sure get that," Gerald said, a look on his face as if he'd known that life.

"So it was just me and the boys drinking and having a good time. Celebrating my big stoppage. After a while, the boys were pretty cockeyed and popping coins into the juke box, trying to get some of the girls to dance. But I was never a dancer. They tried to drag me out there in my sweaty trunks, pulled me by the arms, but I stayed on my stool and kept filling up my glass from the pitchers. So I'm sitting at the end of the bar watching the guys, and out of nowhere this girl appears beside me. Midtwenties, big green eyes, and all this long, dark, curly hair. She had on a tight red leather jacket and a black miniskirt. I asked how she was, and she played with the collar of my robe. Said she caught the fight and wanted to congratulate me. I thought it was a setup by the boys or something, but I looked around, and they were all busy trying to talk up girls around the bar. I moved some coats off the stool next to me, and she sat down and crossed her legs and took a drink outta my beer. Didn't even ask. There was always fire like that in her. And how she looked up at me with the beer in her hand and her eyes all big, this electric wave coming from her and into me. It makes my stomach turn just thinking about it, just telling you the story."

"Even now?" Gerald said.

"People don't have many life-changing moments, do they?"

"I suppose not."

"I know I haven't," Trucks said. He picked up his fork and ate the last few pieces of meat. The elk was cold and soft. He chewed and pictured Elle looking at him with those green eyes. How she'd tilt her head and run her fingers through her curls. He'd seen Claudia do it too. Like one of those things that just passes through blood.

"Well, go on, if you like. I didn't mean to stop you," Gerald said.

"It's just something I haven't thought about in a long time."

Trucks set his fork down and ran his fingers over his knuckles.

"We can save the rest for another time, then, if you don't feel up to it now," Gerald said. "Maybe it's not the right time to talk about it just yet."

Gerald stood and gathered his plate and glass. He took

them over to the sink and set them on the counter. He put a stopper in the drain and turned on the faucet until the sink was half full. Then he set the dishes in the still water.

DISTANT PLACES

It was late in the night. Trucks sat on the floor against the wall. He listened to his girl sleep. He counted punches in his mind, thought about combinations and striking distance. The things he could control.

He tried to distract himself. Rubbed the carpet. Felt the rough glide of it. Pinched little strands between his thumb and middle finger. Every time Claudia twitched or moved or her breathing pattern changed, Trucks would stand and go to her. Hover over the bed like a helpless ghost. He'd touch her chest. Feel the soft beat. Kiss his thumb and run it over her eyebrow. Tell her how sorry he was. Just how fucking sorry. Then he'd sit against the wall again. Exhale. Stare at his knees.

He was back in his old clothes, now clean. Claudia's hung over a chair in the corner of the room. Trucks stood and went over and picked them off the chair. He folded the pajama shirt and set it on the seat. Picked up the bottoms and felt the soft fabric at the cuff. Ran his fingers over the material. Squeezed hard. He folded the bottoms and set them on top of the shirt.

Trucks walked over to his workman's coat hanging on the door handle. He dug through the pockets and grabbed his sachet of antibacterial wipes and a small quarter-full hotel shampoo bottle. He went back to Claudia's bedside and sat on the floor against the wall. He leaned his head back and looked up at the ceiling. The moonlight striking in a light blue. He wondered what it was like to reach such distant places.

He opened the sachet and brought it to his nose. Took a big inhale—gardenia. Claudia had noticed how much it smelled like her mama. Because all Elle ever wore was gardenia perfume. He'd have thought a hooker would have picked something less floral. Less intimate. Opt instead for the kind of smell that would bring on a hard mustang. Not a scent that he'd always remember. That he couldn't let go. And he'd planned to tell Claudia what it was so she'd know her mama smelled of gardenias all the time. That he'd bought a few gardenia plants and carefully taken apart the buds and stems until he had enough petals to cover the entire surface of Elle's bathwater. That he'd drawn a bath for her and sifted the flower petals across the top. Lit soft candles. Waited for her to come back to the old rowhouse they'd rented near the train tracks in Klakanouse. Claudia only four years old at the time, asleep on a pile of blankets in their one shared room. And he waited. And waited. And paced. And waited. And rubbed his knuckles. And waited. Stood for hours fixed at the frigid window. His busted hand on the frame. Whispers of wind coming through the gaps. His broken heart wishing all her excuses weren't lies. That she really was getting hung up at the diner. Working doubles. Covering shifts for sick coworkers. Staying late to wipe down the tabletops and stools and condiment bottles. That she wasn't working the streets again. Blowing some banker in his car. Tugging a dick in a phone booth. Taking it in the ass in the alley behind the convenience store. Spending that moll cash on crushed-up pills she nabbed off forged scrips. Claudia's food and doctor money going up Elle's crooked nose. That nose he'd kiss each night before bed when she actually came back. Her breath smelling like cock and Jack and cigarettes when she forgot to mask it. When she didn't pop a gob of toothpaste in her mouth and swish it before she came home.

Trucks was getting worked up. His heart raced. He set the sachet and tiny shampoo bottle on the dresser next to Claudia's hearing aids. Then he opened the curtain and pulled up the window. He got on his knees and rested his forearms on the sill. He breathed in the harsh night, sweat rolling down his temple. Trucks watched his quick breath go out into nothing.

He wondered how he could have had such deep love for such a messed-up person. And why maybe he loved her still in that back-of-the-mind kind of way. Why he tortured himself carrying around her damn scent all the time. And beat himself up for giving her too many chances. For letting her come back into their lives again and again after every time she disappeared and showed up out of nowhere with another split lip and a thousand sorrys and that goddamn haunting smell of gardenias. And she'd never know about all those nights he'd spent staring out their solitary, frost-covered window wondering if she was even alive or if he'd go out and find her some morning, stiff and blue in a snowbank. Their girl lying curled on the floor. Fingers in her mouth. Full-body breathing the way children do.

Trucks slapped the window sill. Then he did it again.

And again. And again. He'd have punched right through that stubborn window if it weren't for the danger of broken glass. His hands were hot. Red. Stinging and going numb. He looked back at Claudia, but she was still out. Her head to the side. He took one last deep, chilly breath to compose himself. Then he shut the window. He was sick of thinking about the messed-up way he loved people. Like if they didn't break him it wasn't really love.

He grabbed the sachet and closed it up. He decided he'd never tell Claudia what her mama smelled like. Was there a reason to tell her any of it? Did he owe it to her? Wouldn't it just bring some kind of hurt to her like it did him? Punish her every time that smell came around? And she might have the same sickness as Trucks. Walk around with a crushed gardenia flower in her back pocket, folded inside a napkin.

Trucks put the sachet back in the pocket of his coat. Then he returned to the dresser and grabbed the little shampoo bottle. Back at the Archibald Suites he'd dumped the generic hotel shampoo in the toilet and rinsed out the bottle. He'd gone through June's purse while she was passed out and found the onion-shaped perfume bottle. Claudia had been so fond of it. And so fond of June and her kind ways and positive energy. So Trucks poured a bit of the perfume into the shampoo bottle. Figured he'd give it to Claudia as a present. A reminder. Something she could take with her and actually feel good about. Maybe put some on her wrists and neck. Dab it on the "sweet spot" June had shown her. A new smell. New memories.

Trucks set the little bottle on top of the folded pajamas. It'd be waiting there for Claudia when she woke.

Trucks went back to the wall and sat down. He rubbed his eyes and looked at his girl.

"There are no stars, Pepper Flake," he said. But he still couldn't remember the rest of the line. "There are no stars," he said again. And then he drifted off to sleep.

A CHERUB IN BLUE LIGHT

A blue light filled the room, the moon casting strong in the night.

Claudia found Trucks asleep against the wall, hands at his sides, chin against chest, mouth open. He was breathing hard. She got on her knees and looked at the cuts on his face. She reached out and touched them.

Trucks woke. He blinked fast.

Claudia pulled back.

"Pepper Flake?" he said.

"I'm thirsty," she said.

Trucks was trying to orient himself.

"Jesus, I bet," he said. "You must be exhausted."

She pointed to her ears.

Trucks posted on the carpet and stood. Everything was a little hazy. He walked over to the dresser and picked up her hearing aids. He went back to the wall and sat down. Then he said, "I'm gonna put these in, okay?" Then he gently hooked a hearing aid over each of her ears and clicked them on.

"Sound okay?" he asked.

"This one's still blurry," she said.

"I'll figure out how to fix it soon."

"You said that already."

"When we find a real stopping place. Promise."

Claudia didn't look so sure. Trucks was overcome with so much warmth for his girl sitting there in the moonlight. He'd never been so grateful. He wanted to tell her. But he didn't want her to feel overwhelmed by him.

"Where are we?" she asked.

"Montana."

"How'd we get here?"

"A nice man picked us up."

"After you made us leave June?"

Trucks paused. It hurt him to hear it, but it was true. He always tried to make what he thought were the best choices for them. But he could never be sure what was best until later. Much, much later.

"Yes," he said, averting his eyes.

"I don't remember much."

"You were really tired then."

"Yeah."

"And you were mad at me."

"Yeah."

"And now we're here."

"But after June?"

"We walked for a long time in the snow. Do you remember?"

Claudia shook her head.

"Well, we did. And we saw the hills and ridges in the Badlands. Do you remember that?"

She shook her head again.

"I tried to tell you all about them, but it was really cold. And we were both too tired to be walking. And after a while we ran out of steam and fell asleep beside the road."

"And then the man came?"

"And then the man came."

Claudia thought for a while. Trucks was always taken with watching her mind work.

"And now we're in Mown Tinna?" she asked.

"Montana."

"Montana."

"Yeah," he said.

Claudia pulled her knees to her chin. Hugged her legs. She looked at Trucks.

"Are we done hitching?" she asked.

"We should get you into your pajamas," Trucks said.

"I'm okay," she said. "Let's don't move."

"Oh," he said. He was surprised.

Then Claudia scooted closer. She stared at the floor.

"Are you feeling all right?" he asked.

He wanted to reach out, but he was afraid to touch her.

"Still kinda hot."

"You were sleeping for a long time."

"It felt like forever."

He didn't want to say how much it did.

Claudia rocked back and forth.

"How do you feel?" Trucks asked.

"I had nightmares. They were weird and sad."

"You can tell me about them," he said.

"I can't remember much."

"It's okay. Tell me what you feel like."

"Okay." Claudia looked up at the ceiling. "They weren't good."

"I'm sorry. But it's okay to have bad dreams. Life isn't always peaches. That's what the house mother at one of the homes used to tell me. I never really knew what she meant."

"But you do now?" Claudia asked.

"It's just something people say to make themselves feel better about their own lives."

Claudia looked at him. "You were dead in one of the dreams."

"Fuck," Trucks said.

"The swears," she said.

"Sorry. It's just hard to hear."

"I'll stop."

"No. Keep going. Tell me if it'll make you feel better about the dreams."

"I think it will," Claudia said.

"Okay then," Trucks said. He felt sick and helpless.

"I was inside the home, but it was bigger than normal. Like a really big room. And there was a big window I walked up to and could see all the other kids outside. They were smiling and laughing, and people were raking leaves over the kids. I saw Suzie and Mary and Connie playing in the yard, and I wanted to be out there instead of alone inside. But there weren't any doors to get out. There was just the big window and a lot of room inside. So I closed my eyes and hoped for a door to get out. I kept my eyes closed for a long time. It felt like forever, and I kept hoping the whole time. Then when I opened my eyes the big window was gone and there was a door. I ran to the door and opened it, but I couldn't get outside. It was a black closet. You were in there and you were dead. You had white shoelaces around your hands. And when I walked up and pulled on the shoelaces your brains fell out. I felt really sad. You looked like the scarecrow man. And I thought I shouldn't have called you bruiseity brains so much 'cause it was probably my fault your brains got broken and fell out."

Trucks could hardly breathe. What was he doing to her? His eyes stung. He didn't know what to say or what to do. He tried to speak. But all he did was stammer.

Then he started crying. He closed his eyes and put his face in his hands. He felt the hot tears on his cheeks. What had he become? All these breakdowns and emotional rampages. Beyond that. What was he turning her into? All he'd wanted to do was protect her, but now? Wasn't he just messing up her life? Setting her up to be the kind of failure he'd become?

Suddenly a hand pried at his fingers. Trucks looked up. Claudia had his left hand in both of hers. She squeezed it tight and kissed the old, broken thing. He could hardly see her through the haze of tears. All that soft blue light around her. The waves of her curls dark against the glow. She was some kind of angel he didn't deserve. He knew that much. He was determined to do right by her. He'd find a way. He'd really try.

PUZZLE OF AN ALTERNATE UNIVERSE

Claudia sat on the couch in the living room doing a two hundred-piece puzzle and drinking cocoa from a navy mug. Trucks had helped her set the corner pieces and the beginning of an edge. Watched her build on that long wall until her tongue was between her teeth in concentration.

Gerald had made fried eggs, brown rice, and salted tomatoes for breakfast. Trucks had been relieved when Claudia finished her plate and asked for the puzzle. He'd been afraid that the damage from the past few days might have left her unable to function on the basest level.

Trucks watched her now from the kitchen. Admiring her small hands as she worked over the coffee table, putting together that puzzle of a strange and distant universe. Where some planets took the form of strips instead of spheres or radiated pink or were assembled in wavy levels or split down the middle into floating halves. He watched her pick up jagged pieces and place them where they fit. A pile of waiting pieces beside her. He imagined the gears in her mind. Seeing them turn. Click. Run. Work. This precise, little thing he'd created. It touched him always. It really moved him now.

Gerald came back from the fridge and sat across from Trucks at the kitchen table.

"I assume you're feeling some relief now?" Gerald said.

He gestured toward Claudia. The little hotel shampoo bottle of June's perfume sat on the coffee table next to the cocoa mug. Claudia was elated with the surprise. When Trucks had handed it over, she'd opened the bottle and taken a deep inhale, her eyes closed. He could almost feel the hope in her heart. A hint of sadness over having to leave June behind.

"Some. Not as much as you'd think," Trucks said.

"A little guilt, then?"

Gerald slid Trucks the small plate of leftover salted tomatoes. Trucks grabbed a slice.

"More than I've ever experienced," Trucks said. Then he bit into the tomato.

"I understand," Gerald said. "But it seems like you're doing all you can, and what more can a man ask of himself?"

Trucks kept eating the tomato slice. He finished it and grabbed another.

"I've been giving her the best life I can. A roof, food. I've cared for her. I'm no saint, but I think I've done good by her. So we've never gotten outta the gutter, but that doesn't mean I love her less or care less or done less than the middle-class parents. But sure, I feel guilty as hell. And sometimes I feel like trash because I've made my way with my fists and guts instead of typing out reports and tugging a tie. But that wasn't ever supposed to be my life. It wasn't ever me. I never even saw that kind of opportunity. I skipped home to home. Then shelter to shelter. It was a real step when I could afford a place of my own. Like moving up in the sick, forgotten world. But it's really not much of a leap, just moving from the four broken-down walls you're used to to ones you're not. And the place is yours as long as you can keep the landlord off your ass. Don't get behind too much on the rent. Keep the lights on. I used to joke with the boys that it was light outs in the ring, lights on at home."

Trucks paused. He thought about shutting the lights out on all those opponents. *Pah-pah-pah.* Catching each one with the right angle, the quick jab, the looping hook. That ever-calling tingle in his palms when he thought about putting on the old gloves. The feel of the cracking leather. That faded smell. Those old-time babies. He could see the blazing speed of his hands tucked into the gloves like tight pockets. The scent of swift leather when he dug one into the body. *Pah.* When he went to the temple. *Pah.* To the bridge of the nose. *Pah.* Right under the chin so the head snapped back like a limp puppet.

"You okay?" Gerald asked.

Trucks had a faraway look in his eye. He grabbed his glass of water and drank it.

"Yeah," Trucks said.

"You looked pretty lost there," Gerald said.

"Just thinking."

"Hey, I've got a question," Gerald said. "It's not meant to be a prying thing, but I'm curious."

"Okay," Trucks said.

"You didn't say much about taking your daughter when I picked you up, but you said enough. I realize some part of this must be illegal. I don't know. That's not my business, and it's not my question. What I'm wondering is, are you worried? Do you worry they're after you? That they'll come for you? Come looking for her, put you away somewhere? As a father, it's what I'd fear. But I'm not you, and so I'm asking.

I wanna know what that does to you."

Trucks tapped his fingernail against the side of his empty glass. It made a ting noise over and over.

"Our town wasn't so big. Middle of the country. We're just some nobodies from nowhere, and I don't honestly think the state gives two shits about me, her, or what our situation is. They sure didn't care then, and I don't think they'd take the time to care now. I took her from the children's home they were holding her hostage in, if you want the truth. And nothing was worse than that. This life hitching and moving, all the road running, it's no hardship compared to being without her. Knowing she was spending every minute with strangers, trapped in some rickety house and wondering if she'd ever see me again. No, Gerald. I don't fear that at all. Maybe they put something in the paper. Maybe it's even been on the local news. I really don't know. But how often do you see poor kids on the TV? Never. What you see is the golden children of the wealthy. Those are the only ones they care about losing. Anyway. The more miles I put between us and all those old memories, the better it is for me and her. And that's all my life's gonna be about now, is what's best for her and what I can make for us."

Trucks stared off again. He turned the empty glass.

"You're a good man. I wouldn't make your kinda decisions, but it doesn't mean I don't admire what you're doing, because I know it's out of love and deep care. That's easy to see. We don't all go about it the same, but that you're going about it at all, well, that's the thing that matters." Gerald paused. "So what were you thinking of earlier when you had that look in your eye?"

Trucks grabbed another tomato slice. He scraped off the salt. Then he set the slice back down on his plate. He looked over at Claudia. She was sitting on the couch with her legs folded to one side, leaning on her forearm and moving puzzle pieces around. She didn't look bored. Just concentrating. Intense.

"What have you loved in life you just couldn't shake?" Trucks asked. "I could explain it better, but I think you'll know what I mean."

Gerald took a sip of coffee. Some egg scraps on his plate. His fork askew. He was deep in thought.

"You don't have to answer," Trucks said. "Maybe it was a stupid question."

Trucks stood and walked over to the sink. He filled his water glass and chugged until it was gone. Then he looked out the little window at the surrounding acreage. Watched the gray morning sky hovering over Crow Agency like a descending blanket.

"I'd say my wife," Gerald said. "But I don't know if you can really count that. She wasn't something you'd want to 'shake,' as you put it. Because the things you wanna shake are the things that feel like small drips of poison. Those things you return to again and again when half your gut says no and the other half thinks you couldn't live another day without it. And then you wonder, is it actually love when it comes to those things? Is it love or sickness or addiction or some kind of consolation for a different life you can't have? Can't make? Even with the greatest of intentions and will? Hell if I know."

Trucks half-filled his glass with water. He walked over to

the table and sat down.

"Were you born to love her? Your wife? Do you think you were made to know each other like that?" Trucks asked.

Gerald grabbed his fork and scraped the egg debris on his plate. Then he looked up. "The way we fit together and the strength of our love, you'd be dumb not to at least consider it. Like you're walking this big open country for all these years and meet all these people that are nice enough but make you think *stranger, stranger, stranger, stranger*. None of them feeling enough like you or your kind. None of them making the fit. Then one day you meet her, and within a minute, you're not thinking *stranger*. You're thinking, *Girl, I know you. I've known you all along.*"

Trucks took a bite of the scraped-off tomato.

"It sounds too good to be real," Trucks said.

"It's an uncommon feeling, I think," Gerald said. "Lots of people talk about it, saying they were made for each other, but those are the same idiots you find divorced in two years. Words get thrown around a lot. Notions about romance plugged into their heads through the TV and the magazines. But it ain't real love. Not even close to that deep, unending thing that so few have. That's how I see it, anyhow. That's my dime's worth."

"What about your kids? Could you say that with them too? That you knew them all along?"

Gerald thought. Trucks finished the tomato. The plate was empty now.

"No. Not with the children. They came from me. I made them. The similarities were implied in the making. Me and my kids might not be the exact same or even all that similar

sometimes, like with my oldest, Josie. She can't stand being in nature. She always hated the homestead here, hauling
feed to the horses and pigs and cows and chickens. Camping
out in the sticks and trudging through shit and getting up
at first light and all the good stuff that comes with this life.
But we're still made of the same blood. And with Maddie,
my wife, she was no part of my blood but every part of my
being. That's the best I could put it, I guess."

Trucks ran his fingertips over his glass.

"That's definitely not a sickness," Trucks said.

"No, it's not. It's a truly beautiful thing." Gerald looked
out the window. "I already assume the answer, but have you
had it? You felt anything like that solid, endless love?"

Trucks put his hand under the table. He ran his knuckles
along the underside of the hard wood.

"Nothing like you described, no. With Elle and me, it
was always like a sickness. I'd get worried when she'd leave
for days all strung out. Not knowing if she was bent on pills
or heroin. Afraid when she returned that she'd only leave
again. And me always fearing that final leaving. Every day
just fearing it like a ghost of fire you either walk through or
put out. Boy, I don't miss being sick like that. The helpless-
ness in your gut. Always trying to explain to my little girl
where her mama was. Why she wasn't home for breakfast,
for dinner, for playing time in the alley. How can you be
right with yourself if all you're doing is lying to your kid?
And how long can a man keep that up before he breaks?
Or before it breaks his girl? But even in my moments of
sickness—my girl in the tub or sleeping on the floor or col-
oring in a book, her mama out somewhere doing all those

crooked things—it kinda lit me up. Made me feel sparked and alive. Like being left is the only way I know how to love and live. And you find a way to deal. Always has to be some kind of outlet for that pain and loss. And even when I was young and going home to home, I still had the gym. The ring. And you can move all you want between those ropes, pedal for miles and miles, but that ring goes nowhere. And the scars pile up. The bleeds. The bruises. The breaks. But that boxing doesn't save you. It's temporary. It's just the salve on the wound that tears a little each day, and all you're try- ing to do is get it closed, pull it closed, keep it closed. But it's never easy as that. Nothing is. And one day she leaves and never turns back. And you've got your girl still, but you also have all these piling bills. Because the winter's not get- ting any warmer, and the fights don't come any faster, and the purses don't grow any larger. And one day you lose your girl. They take her from you. Then you lose your mind. And while your mind is lost you try to work through everything you knew then and everything you know now, and the only thing you work out is that you're a man. You're a man with a good chin whose been taking shots for years, and this ain't any different if you don't allow it to be. So you live with the lights out, and you eat next to nothing, and you take your plastic bucket to make cowboy showers in the convenience store restroom, and you say yes to the promoters fucking you over with small purses because you've got nothing left but to get your girl back. And you get evicted and sleep on the streets and tuck away under bridges but keep saving your stashed money in a rusted-out coffee tin and hide it at the back end of a fire escape between Rosemont and Ferry right

near where you met the woman who'd rather live to die by
the eye of a needle than raise the precious thing you'd made
together. And so you take all you have in the pit of you and
roll up your sickness and anger and poison and hate and take
it out on those fights and land the drifting punches and run
when you have to and absorb when you can't and feel the
bang and the thump and the spin of lights when you take
that real pop, and at some point you've stuffed enough away
in that metal can that you can find some forgiveness in laying that money down to the sharks before they fuck up your
knees or your back and you find your way to that goddamn
children's home and grab your girl and say without saying
that *this* is what it means to care about someone, that *this*
is what a man does, that *this* is all you can do and all you've
ever done, and good enough or not, it must stand because
you've got nothing left and no other way to make it in this
crazy world of yours and that one day she'll know that and
must know that by the beating your face has taken and the
crooked fingers you've held her with for so damn long that
they're molded to her feel like a quiet prayer of forgiveness
or a touch like the mantra *to never let go.*"

TWO FOR SPLITTING

Trucks had given Claudia a hatchet with a leather sheath over the blade. It was like an axe to her proportions. He showed her the motion. The dominant hand at the top. The other steady and firm at the bottom. He demonstrated how to position the legs as a base, lift the axe, bring it down with a slide of the top hand. Crack.

"Good. But when you come down, slide that lead hand along the wood," Trucks said. He came up behind her and took her arms. He could smell June's perfume. "Up, like this. Then use those little lats to do the work. Legs rooted. And come down like a pendulum."

Claudia giggled. "That's a funny word."

Trucks stepped away. "Give it a try by yourself. Not fast. Just like we practiced."

Claudia stepped up to the chopping block. Raised the little hatchet. Came down with better form. More control.

"See, that's a good one," Trucks said.

"Better?"

"A lot better, Pepper Flake. You're getting it."

Claudia smiled.

"Let's see it a few more times," he said.

"Okay."

She brought the hatchet up. Slow. Even. Her breath flowing out in little clouds. Came down with the hatchet. She looked over at Trucks, and he nodded. She took the hatchet up again, then back down.

"How about we get that sheath off and have you split a real piece of wood?"

"I guess so," Claudia said.

She handed over the hatchet, and Trucks unsnapped the leather sheath. He put the sheath in his coat pocket and inspected the blade. He handed it over to Claudia.

"I like that it's shiny and pretty," she said.

"It might look pretty, but it's dangerous. It's killing sharp, so be careful. Be gentle. Don't take your eye off it. Okay?"

"Okay," she said. She fixated on the blade.

"Just stand there and hang on."

Trucks grabbed a half log from the unsplit pile, whittled down to nothing much after his feverish chopping that first morning. He walked back over and put the half log on the chopping block.

"Now measure that distance," he said. "You remember how?"

Claudia held the hatchet out with both hands. She looked at Trucks for confirmation.

"Don't look at me. Watch your blade. Line up the cut."

Claudia looked back at the wood. The tip of the blade was at the center. She hesitated. She shook.

"What?" Trucks asked.

She relaxed her arms and looked over at him.

"I don't wanna break it," she said.

"The axe?"

"No, the wood. It looks nice when it's not broken."

Trucks walked over. He held out his hand, and she gave

him the hatchet. He snapped the leather sheath back on and set the hatchet beside the piece of half wood on the chopping block. He picked her oversized gloves up out of the snow and put them on Claudia's hands. Then he walked over to the unsplit pile and covered it with a small tarp. When he turned around, she was standing behind him. Following him like a small shadow.

"Here," he said, and held out his hand.

She looked confused. Almost reluctant. But she took his hand, and he walked her away from the woodpile and the covered blades. They went down a winding slope that led to the horse pasture. Wooden fences with thick, knotted slats ran for hundreds of yards around the field.

Trucks pulled his coat sleeves over his cold bare hands and brushed snow off the top wooden rail. Then he blew into his hands and picked Claudia up and placed her on the rail. She rested her feet on the middle slat. Trucks stood beside her. Leaned his elbows on the top rail. They looked out at this new big-sky world.

"This is where the horses used to run," he said. "Back when Gerald was keeping horses."

Claudia leaned in to him. She pointed to her ears, and said, "The wind's loud."

Trucks reached in her hood, behind her ears, and slightly turned the volume dials down. First the left, then the right.

"That better?" he asked.

"Yeah," she said.

Trucks went back to leaning on the railing. "So I said this is where the horses used to run back when Gerald was keeping them."

"Where did he keep them?"

"See the barn over there? The one with the open doors?"

"Yup."

"He used to keep them there in the stalls. Feed them oats and hay."

"They probably didn't like it there. Horses are sposed to run around."

"You're right."

"I like when their long hair bounces when they run. Did he have more animals?"

"Chickens, cows, pigs. Probably some goats, I'd guess. I don't know."

"My friend Mary said chickens are mean and they poke you if you bother them."

"Peck," he said.

"Peck," she said.

"And I don't think they peck you on purpose to be cruel or anything. They seem to peck at about anything solid or anything that looks like food—pebbles, grains, seed, grass, scraps. Like they're nothing more than scavengers."

"I'd probably run if I saw them."

"You don't have to worry. There aren't any here. And I'm with you, besides."

Claudia didn't say anything. She kicked her heels against the wood and looked forward.

"Where did the horses go? Did they jump over the fence and run away?" she asked.

"I don't know where they went. Gerald felt too old to farm, I guess. Or maybe he didn't have the heart for it anymore. It takes a lot of work to run an animal family."

"Do you think the horses ran away?"

"I don't know. Probably not. Why do you think they'd do that?"

"The fence," she said. Like it was the most obvious thing.

"Oh," he said. And thought about it. "You probably have a point."

"If they put me in a fence, I'd jump over it and run away too. That's what I think. And if you're as fast and big as a horse, you can run far and get away from everyone and be strong if anything tries to hurt you. But I wouldn't wanna have to run. I'd rather stay and be nice with everyone than have to leave."

Trucks folded his hands together. Looked at them. Then he said, "Nothing's gonna hurt you, Pepper Flake."

Claudia looked away. She stared beyond the pasture for a while. Then she swung her legs over the top rail and jumped down.

"I'm gonna go inside," she said.

She started walking toward the house.

"Hey," Trucks yelled.

Claudia turned around.

"Don't you believe me?"

Claudia shrugged.

"I swear on everything, nothing's gonna hurt you."

"You can't say promises like that," Claudia said, and then she turned and kept walking.

Trucks watched her go up the incline. Smooth. Quick. No bit of hesitation. And under her breath, as she moved farther and farther away, he could have sworn he heard her little voice: "You can't. You just can't."

THE PONDEROSA CONFERENCE

The three of them laid in the dark under a tall ponderosa pine. They all had their hoods up, using them like thin pillows. Claudia was in the middle. They were looking at the night sky. Gerald pointed out the constellations they could see and traced the ones they couldn't. Trucks listened. He had no idea about astronomy and the patterns of stars. He knew only the patterns of punches—how to throw them, how to dodge them, how to absorb them. As Gerald talked, Trucks closed his eyes and thought of all the galaxies he must have drawn with his fists. How many times he'd seen stars after a nasty pop. Maybe, in his current life, he was a planet, Claudia the moon. Ever circling each other but always this gap. Like the dark chasm could never be crossed.

Trucks opened his eyes. They adjusted to the night sky. He grabbed for Claudia's hand, but she pulled away and put her big-gloved hands on her stomach. She breathed a big sigh.

"Where did your wife go?" Claudia asked Gerald.

"Well, she died," he said. "Part of that cycle we all must complete."

"Do you miss her?" she asked, turning to him.

"Of course I do. It was really tough losing her."

Claudia turned back to look at the sky. There was silence

for a while.

"And she's up there somewhere with the people in the constant-ations?"

Trucks didn't correct her.

Gerald said, "That's a nice way to think of it. Yeah. Sure she is."

"So I was right?" Claudia said.

Gerald thought a moment. "You carry the people you lose with you in some capacity or another. When their body calls it quits, the spirit goes floating. Maddie, my wife, she's spread out there over the hill of flowers." He raised his arm and pointed with his thumb. "I could show you if it was spring and they were all blooming. You couldn't see her, of course. Not like she was. She's part of that soil now. She's among the flowers. In the roots and stems and petals. She's feeding the world in her way, and that's beautiful, see?"

Claudia nodded.

"I used to show her the constellations too. We'd come lay out here and trace from star to star, light to light, until we thought we got them all. But I bet there's far more out there we can't even see. There's so much we just don't know. We can only see what's visible to us or what our minds allow. So some of where you see those people you lost is in the things you used to do together, the sounds and feels and smells of the world that give you the reminders of the ones you loved. Even the feel of this snow on my back, the way I see a napkin folded, the smell of lilac, reading the words *star anise*, or a pair of rainboots in a storefront window. Memories, I guess. Private and very personal reminders of who they were and the life you had together. It only means something to you.

It's only true of love and loss from your view. In your mind.
In that little spinning universe you got right up there." Gerald lightly tapped on his head. "And it's all yours. It's what
you've created. What you've made of it."

The three of them kept looking up. Their breaths coming
out at opposite intervals.

Gerald grabbed the cuff of Claudia's coat and tugged
on it. "How do you feel about heading out tomorrow?" he
asked. Trucks had told Gerald it would be best if they left
soon. He didn't feel good about leaning on Gerald like they
had. Gerald offered another day or two, but Trucks already
felt guilty enough.

"Okay, I guess," Claudia finally said.

"Got everything packed?" Gerald asked, though they had
next to nothing.

"I guess. It's getting easy."

"How so?"

"We've done it a lot. It feels normal kinda."

"I bet you've met some nice people."

"Yeah."

"And soon you'll be in a fresh city with lots of new people
and adventures and some nice friends to play with. You'll be
the little traveler girl with the cool boxing daddy. You'll have
so many stories for your friends that talking to you will be
like a magical story time for them."

Claudia smiled. "I didn't think of it like that." She pulled
on her left hearing aid and scratched her ear.

"How many of those kids went all the way across the
country just to live somewhere new?"

"Probably not any."

"Exactly. You'll be a cool bean in your new place."

"I just don't want them to make fun of me and my hearing phones." She reached up and covered her ears.

"Oh, kid," Gerald said. He reached over and patted her shoulder.

Trucks rubbed Claudia's forearm with the back of his hand.

"Will I be weird 'cause I came from so far?" she asked.

"I don't think so," Gerald said. "I think the kids will find you interesting. They'll want to listen to your stories. So the hearing aids make you a bit different from the other kids. That's okay. It's not a bad thing to be your own person. There's nothing wrong in being what you are and finding a common ground with others. Be good. Be nice. Be generous. The kids will respond."

Claudia put her hands on her stomach and sighed.

"Okay," she said. "I hope it's true."

"Only way to find out is to go, huh?" Gerald said.

Claudia sighed again.

Trucks reached for her hand. This time she let him hold on. He gave her fingers a nice squeeze and let go. It was funny feeling her little hands beneath those old gloves of his. He wanted to hold on longer, but that small connection was enough for now.

"Who else's butt's getting cold?" Gerald asked.

"Mine!" Claudia said.

"Maybe we should head in. I can scavenge some logs, crank the fireplace."

Claudia turned to Gerald. "What happens when the logs go to the fireplace?"

Gerald looked at the sky. "Up through the chimney, and then they become stars."

THE REAL DARK

Trucks spent the night lying on the floor beside the bed. Claudia was tucked in the sheets, sleeping hard after sitting in front of the fire. Trucks didn't mind the stiff carpet under his back. Having a roof meant everything. He'd spent many of those hours at the kitchen table, sitting in the dim light. A map spread out. He thought about how Gerald had talked about Montana, a nice place to raise a child, good people, beautiful land. That maybe Trucks could learn a new way of life for himself and offer Claudia an entirely different world. Far from anything she'd known. But there was a pull in Trucks. A burn deep down that said he was his own man and Nevada was where he could find quick action. Take fast fights. Pocket some okay purses until he rose up the ranks. Made the real bills. This thing his mind and body and spirit understood so well. Adrift in his blood. So much a part of his making that he didn't know who he was without it.

Trucks stared at the ceiling. He missed the soft blue glow from the other night. It was dark tonight. That true dark that makes a man look hard into himself. The kind of dark that brings that acidic fear of death to the mind. Like it could happen at any moment. The way he felt carrying his girl through the Badlands. The harsh cries of winter. How it burned against his skin.

He was suddenly too aware of his heartbeat. Of Claudia's

breathing. That gentle *hiiiii-haaaaa* he'd come to know so well over the years. The two of them alone in that shack of an apartment in Klakanouse. Taking care of her since she was a baby. Elle never had the instincts of a mother. Refused to breast feed. Unwilling to coddle. She'd even held Claudia with a gap between them, like if they ever fully touched she could never rid herself of the little girl. And so Elle was gone and gone and gone. Would sometimes roll back through the doorway like a drugged-up yo-yo. Return only for something she'd forgotten—hidden cash or uppers or needles or whatever she was hiding in all those inconvenient places. The return always so short. Leaving that faint gardenia smell like a whisper. Haunting him. Like maybe she'd never really been there. Or, when it lingered long enough, make him think she actually might return.

He kept staring at the ceiling. Putting one fist into his palm, then switching. Back and forth all night. He tried to think of what was best for Claudia. There were guaranteed fights in Nevada. He was assured of it by the boys. But for the first time his mind was heavy with the idea that he had to seek different movement and a new way to provide. That maybe the hitching and boxing wasn't best for his girl. Conflicting. How something so deep in his blood could hurt someone so dear to him. Trucks tried to think of Nevada in another way. Maybe he didn't have to be the one taking the punishment. He could coach or corner or cut. But could it bring the kind of peace he'd hoped for? Or should he listen to Gerald and stick it out in Montana?

Trucks was reminded of the map he'd spread on the table that night. The US guidebook Gerald had shown him before he went to bed. Trucks had studied the map hard. Followed its veins of roads with a finger. He looked at the city dots spread over the map like stars. He imagined them as different lives he and Claudia could have. Walking harbors in Portsmouth. Getting ice cream in Davis. Scaling red rocks in West Valley. Dipping shrimp in Goose Creek. Lives of light and adventure, not just scraping by. Not just surviving. But it was nothing but fantasy. He knew. And if the choice was going to be about her, then he needed to narrow it down to something practical that might last, that could actually work. If they were sticking to Montana or heading to Nevada, the direction was the same; they'd take 90 West. He thought about the towns he'd checked off in his mind while thumbing the map, measuring the route to Billings. Only an hour away. A northwest trajectory. Dunmore to Hardin to Toluca to Indian Arrow. Wouldn't even take long to hitch up there. Probably find a ride real quick. Especially if they started in the early morning. And if things didn't work out in Billings, couldn't they just roll on down the highway? It's not like 90 West ended there. It's not like anything had to.

Trucks sat up. He figured it was three in the morning. He stood and looked at Claudia as she slept. The smell of June's perfume hung light in the air. He wondered if it was a mistake to have given her the bottle, but what was done was done. He'd tucked Claudia in tight at bedtime, but now the blanket and sheets were off her. Her body askew. He pulled the blanket up over her and patted it down around the crooks of her.

"Montana or Nevada, Pepper Flake? What do you think?"

Trucks walked over to the bedroom door, took his workman's coat off the handle, slipped it on, and left the room. He quietly walked through the house until he got to the front door. Trucks slipped on his boots and went outside.

He walked into the real dark. The wind zipped hard. Trucks put his hands in his coat pockets and bounced up and down in the yard. He looked out at the world coming into its birth. Heard the pine branches shaking in the breeze.

His mind said, Dunmore to Hardin to Toluca to Indian Arrow.

His heart said, *Pah-pah-pah-pah.*

Dunmore to Hardin to Toluca to Indian Arrow.

Pah-pah-pah-pah.

Dunmore to Hardin to Toluca to Indian Arrow.

Pah-pah-pah-pah.

Dunmore to Hardin to Toluca to Indian Arrow.

Pah-pah-pah-pah.

MEADOWLARK VS. CUTTHROAT

The food and rest and warmth had raised her spirit. Claudia was close to good again.

The three of them were in the sun room. It was morning. Trucks and Gerald sat at the small oak table. Claudia stood near the window. She had one hand pressed against the glass, the other holding June's perfume. She watched the white world outside.

Gerald had set a navy duffel bag on the table. He offered it to Trucks as a gift to replace the torn plastic Hallowell sack he'd been using to carry their food and supplies. He'd filled the duffel bag with oranges, bananas, apples, peanut butter, crackers, water bottles, puzzle books, a roadmap, and metal cutlery. Trucks hardly knew what to say. Gerald was such a good and thoughtful man.

Trucks was torn about what to do next. The fire in him wanted to hitch toward Nevada where he could pick up quick work training boxers or cornering other fighters. The more sensible part of him knew it was probably better for his girl to be rooted someplace calm and simple where not a word of boxing was ever uttered.

Claudia turned from the window and shook out the hand that had been touching the glass. "It's freezing," she said.

Gerald laughed. "What'd you expect, little one?"

Claudia shrugged. Then she rubbed the little shampoo bottle in her hands.

"You think you should put that in your coat pocket so you don't lose it?" Trucks said.

"I wanna hold it," she said. Then she looked down at the bottle. "I like to hold it."

"Okay," he said.

"Where would you wanna go if you could go anywhere?" Gerald asked her.

"I don't know. What are the good places? I wanna go to the good places," Claudia said.

"What do you think of it here so far?" Gerald asked.

"Mown Tinna?"

Gerald laughed. "Yeah."

Claudia sat down at the table. She rocked the little shampoo bottle.

"I know you haven't been here long," Gerald said, "but I was wondering. I've been trying to convince your father to stick around."

"It's nice, I think. But really cold. I love the big fields and trees and the smell of wood and stuff. You said they have lots of animals and pretty flowers. I like that."

"Sharp girl. It's certainly beautiful here. Nobody could doubt that," Gerald said.

Claudia tossed the shampoo bottle in the air and caught it. She kept doing that.

"Maybe I should hold that so you don't lose it," Trucks said.

"I won't lose it," she said.

"It seems to mean a lot to you," Gerald said.

"Yeah," she said. Then she closed one eye and looked at the bottle real close. "Yeah, I like it a lot."

"You didn't put any on this morning," Trucks said.

"I wanna save it," she said. Then she put it in her pocket like he'd told her earlier. "June said it was for important things. I wanna keep it important. And there's not even much left."

Trucks hadn't taken much from June's onion-shaped bottle. He didn't want her to notice any was missing. He admired that Claudia was so thoughtful about saving the scent and using it when it mattered. But then he wondered what mattered to Claudia. What it'd take for her to think something was important or valuable. He always questioned his worth with her.

"So what's it gonna be?" Gerald asked Trucks. "You gonna let me take you up to Billings, or are you gonna be stubborn about it? I know you've got your own way of doing things and probably want to continue on, hitching or whatever, but I'm offering."

Bolts of thought flashed through Trucks's mind. The hitching and the boxing and the possibility of going clean for his girl. He wanted to make it simple and safe for her, but he also wanted to live on his own terms. They could only accept help for so long.

"I was thinking it through last night," Trucks said.

"Figure anything out?" Gerald asked.

Trucks looked at Claudia. She was fidgeting with the bottle in her pocket.

"You know, I've got this old gambling token," Gerald said. He pulled the token from his pocket and held it between his thumb and forefinger. "It's special to Montana and can only be used here in the state. Anyhow, maybe we could flip it? Make it easier on you. Meadowlark, I take you up to Billings, drop you off, and you consider sticking around. Cutthroat," Gerald turned the coin over, "and I drop you at the closest on-ramp and let you keep hitching. Up to you. Just thought I'd throw it out there. Anyhow, fifty-fifty ain't bad odds."

Trucks looked at Claudia. She nodded.

"All right," Trucks said.

"Let's have the little miss do the flipping," Gerald said.

Gerald handed Claudia the token. She scooted back her chair and stood. Then she held her breath and flipped the token in the air. They watched it turn over and over. Arcing up and up until it came back down and clanged on the floor. It spun a while before it stopped.

"Goddamn meadowlark," Trucks said.

DREAMER DECEIVER

Claudia played with her toast at Hammy's Diner in Billings. She cut off little pieces and pushed them around her plate.

"Eat it, don't mess around," Trucks said. "You know how many people are out there starving to death, bare bones and begging?"

"Sorry," Claudia said.

"We're lucky to have this meal," Trucks said.

Claudia looked down, twisted a piece of toast in the syrup, and took a bite.

Trucks drank his lemon water, looked at Gerald, and shook his head.

"Not a lot of chance for a kid to be a kid sometimes," Gerald said. "And I mean no offense by it. But you've both lived a tough one."

Gerald picked up his coffee to take a sip. He realized it was empty. He signaled the waitress, and she brought more.

"For us it's never been a clean, easy life. Every move is hard and precise, each meal for a reason, not just because it's that time of the day. I've tried to give her joy and laughter, but survival comes first. And how many people are really out there only surviving? It's few. It's a small margin. It's not how I wanted it for her, but it's how it is with us right now.

Guess it's always how it's been. I'm looking for better. I'm working on it." Trucks looked at Claudia beside him. Ran a hand through her hair. Looked back at Gerald. "It all has to be for something."

Gerald nodded. He scraped some beans off his plate. Then he mixed them with his runny eggs and took a bite.

"It looks like a decent town from what I saw coming in," Trucks said. He took a bite of hash browns and looked at Claudia. She stopped playing around and took a bite too. "What do you think so far, Pepper Flake?"

Claudia shrugged. With her mouth full, she said, "In more days I could know."

"See, there you go," Gerald said. He tapped Claudia on the wrist. "I think that's the best idea. Get your bearings. Find a warm place to stay. Wander the town. You'll find a bunch of friendly faces around here. People who'll stop and help. Who care. You can trust me on that. I've spent a good deal of time here. It's the big city in this area, especially when you consider a town as small as out where I live." Gerald laughed. "Me and Maddie used to bring the kids up here for the strawberry festival. Thousands and thousands of strawberries and strawberry cakes and creams and pies and, oh boy. Everybody dressed in red and white. A play area for the kids. Face painters. Balloons. Arts and crafts and the like. Our kids just really ate it up. Some people get so into it they show up in full round strawberry costumes. Wandering the festival like a big padded fruit. Ha! It really gets me. And they also do a Custer's Last Stand Reenactment, and that's a real holler. Dressed up in full attire with gun smoke and screaming Indians, reenacting the whole Battle of Little Big

Horn. The actual battlefield's near my homestead, believe it or not. From the look on your face, I should shut up. I just love this state, what this whole area has to offer. I'm done. I can be done with it now, promise."

"It's my interested face. You don't have to quit talking," Trucks said.

"I know I get going sometimes, and Maddie used to have a hell of a time slowing down this barreling train."

"I can imagine," Trucks said. He finished his hash browns. Scraped up the last bits of egg until he'd cleaned his plate. Then he reached over and took a few strips of bacon from a pile in the center of the table.

"Finish your milk," Trucks said to Claudia.

She took the glass and chugged the milk. Some if it ran down her face.

"And wipe your chin, knucklehead," Trucks said.

"Everybody about done here?" Gerald asked.

Trucks looked at Claudia. She'd finished her toast and oatmeal. It made him proud that she understood the value of not wasting anything.

"Looks like it," Trucks said.

"Let's go to the strawberry fair," Claudia said.

Gerald laughed. "Not until the summer, little one."

"I'll pay our share when the check comes," Trucks said. He still had a chunk of the thirty dollars he'd brought from Wisconsin.

"Took care of it already when you two were in the bathroom washing up. I'm old. I got money to spend. You two need to save all you can."

"Dammit," Trucks said. But he felt relieved. "I appreciate

it, but you gotta stop being so generous."

"Better than spoiling the hell outta my grandkids. Like they need any more of that."

Trucks pulled the sachet out of his coat pocket. He handed an antibacterial wipe to Claudia and took one for himself. He offered one to Gerald.

"It's good to keep the skin clean. Kills the germs and bacteria. I got tired of battling colds when training for fights. My immune system would break down, even in top shape."

Gerald took an antibacterial wipe from the sachet.

"And what kinda shape are you in now?" Gerald asked.

"I guess okay. Not great. I had to go up and down weight classes a lot to pick up enough fights to pay off my bills and get this little haymaker back," Trucks said. He nudged Claudia.

"Hey," she said. "You watch it." She gave a fake scowl.

They cleaned their hands with the wipes and left them on their plates. Trucks put the big gloves on Claudia, pulled her hood up, closed her throat flaps, and snapped them in place. He shouldered the duffel bag, and the three of them walked out the door.

They crossed the street to Gerald's pickup. He got down on a knee so he could be face-to-face with Claudia.

"Well. You sure are a good little bean," Gerald said.

"And you sure are the nicest old man," Claudia said.

"Ha. Who you calling old?"

"You!"

"Well, it's true, I guess. Wish I had your youth."

"But at least you got your wife at home when the flowers come out."

Gerald's lip quivered. He gave Claudia a big hug.

"I'll miss you and think of you," he said, his chin on her shoulder. "Listen to your daddy. He's a strong man. A tough man. He'll be there for you."

"Okay," she said. The two of them separated. Before Gerald could stand, Claudia held a hand out for him to stop. Then she reached in her pocket and pulled out June's perfume. She opened it up, dipped a little on her finger, and tapped it to both sides of his neck.

"Now you can smell pretty when you get home and remember us," she said.

Gerald hugged her again. Then he stood, wiped his eyes, and put his hand out to Trucks. Trucks gave Gerald a firm handshake.

"Well, it's been good getting to know you. I enjoyed our talks. You ever make it back my way, come down the lane and see me. My door's open to you both. Remember, chin down in the ring, chin up in life. You can thank the Sisters of St. Agnes of Latah County for that one."

Trucks smiled and stepped back. Gerald got into his big pickup and shut the door. Then he cranked down the window.

"Here," he said to Claudia. "Open your hands."

She put her hands out. Gerald dropped the gambling token into her palms.

"A souvenir. Sometimes, you just have to make your own luck. Enjoy Billings. Chins up."

Gerald smiled, rolled up the window, and started the engine. He waved and took off down the road. Soon he turned a corner, and they were alone again.

Trucks stood still. Claudia flipped the coin. Up in the air. Down on the ground.

Fwup. Cling. Fwup. Cling. Fwup. Cling. Fwup. Cling.

"I wanna get the fish, but it keeps landing on the bird," she said.

"What's that?"

"It keeps landing on the bird," she said again. "I can't get the fish."

"Let me see that," Trucks said.

He took the coin and flipped it in the air. Let it hit the ground. He tried over and over. He gave it back to Claudia, and she tried it over and over too. Always the same result. A trick coin.

"Goddamn meadowlark," Trucks said.

Fwup. Cling.

OUTSIDE THE BEARTOOTH RESCUE MISSION

Trucks and Claudia sat on a bench facing the street. They were both thinking of Gerald, missing him in different ways.

"We can go in and give it a shot," Trucks said. "Your choice."

They watched cars pass. People walked by, sometimes looking over and smiling in that guilty kind of way.

"Maybe here's better. The last couple times hitching wasn't good," she said. "We fell asleep in the snow. And lots of times people don't stop."

"Sometimes they're just busy with their own lives. And a lot of people fear hitchers."

"Why?"

"The movies and magazines. And society tells them to be afraid."

"But why?"

"Fear the outcasts. I don't know. It's just something society spreads around. Be afraid of what's different. Reject the things that aren't like you. You can imagine how many messed-up looks I got when I told people I was a boxer. Some would even take a step back when I said it, like all I knew how to do was hurt people."

Trucks looked at his hands on top of the duffel bag in his lap.

"Live our way, or else. That's what society says, Pepper Flake."

"Or else what?"

"Nothing. Just remember, don't listen to them. Listen to you. Listen to me. You bring enough tight people into your life and that's your own little society. You can trust each other. Believe in each other. And I got you now, and that's enough for me. When I think of it, it's always been all the people I needed. Just you," he said.

Trucks looked at her, but she was staring into the street.

"You know what I mean?"

"Yeah," Claudia said. She closed her eyes. "But what about 'or else?' Or else what happens if you don't do what society says?"

"Let's not talk about it now."

"Fine." Claudia looked at Trucks. "Who's society?"

"Not us," Trucks said.

"What happens in the shelter?" Claudia asked.

"I guess you don't remember the times we were in and out when you were younger? Back in Wisconsin?"

Claudia shook her head.

"Not at all?" Trucks asked.

"No."

"Before we rented the little rowhouse?"

"No."

"Guess you were too small to remember."

"I spose."

"Well, think of it like the children's home, except there's all kinds of people, not just kids. A lot of them smell bad. They've got it real tough. A lot of them are older men. You know, with the gray beards and dirty skin. You saw them all over the old neighborhood."

"I remember the bad smells. Maybe I could give them some of the perfume. Would it be good to do that?"

"It'd be kind, Pepper Flake, but I think you should save it for yourself. If you gave it out to every hard case, you wouldn't have any left."

"Okay."

"But the idea's nice. It's a good one. Like you. You're a real good one, you know that?"

Claudia swung her feet under the bench and back. Trucks gave her neck a light squeeze.

"Will we keep moving places?" she asked.

"I don't know. It's up to how things go, I guess."

"Yeah."

"How do you want them to go?" he asked.

She didn't say anything. Trucks gently pulled her arm to look at him. He adored Claudia hidden under her hood, the throat flaps tight against her.

"You can answer. It's okay," he said.

"I want them to go so you don't die and I don't have bad dreams anymore and we never fall asleep on the road. And I wanna meet friends like Suzy and Mary and Connie 'cause they're far away now and probably don't miss me like I miss them sometimes. Cause there were a lot of other kids at the home, and they probably play with them now."

Trucks dug his knuckles into his thigh. He scanned the street. Felt the sting of winter.

"I'll do all I can to make that happen for you," he said. "And I hope you know that. And I hope you know I'm trying hard. The things we ask for don't always happen. Sometimes we get them, and we thank the world for working in our favor. But it's not often like that for people like us. So remember there are hard times, and those are the usual times. That's what you're already used to. And you need to keep getting used to it. But it doesn't mean we can't still try for the better times. All the hard times make the better times that much sweeter."

"I wish it was always the better times," Claudia said. She leaned back on the bench.

"I'll do all I can to give you the better. I can't guarantee anything but my trying. I hope that's enough."

They were quiet for a while. The wind was calm. Traffic lights blinked. Cars rolled along. Pedestrians walked quickly past the shelter.

"So we sleep here?" she asked.

"Only if you're up for it."

Claudia pulled the gambling token from her coat pocket. She looked at its copper surface.

"Do you feel better when we stay or when we go?" he asked.

Claudia shrugged. She had a faraway look he couldn't read.

"It's hard to know," she said. "It hurts both ways."

INSIDE THE BEARTOOTH RESCUE MISSION

"We've got eighty-two beds in the men's shelter and seventy-one in the women and children's shelter," said the woman at intake.

"What about meals?" Trucks asked.

"We do three a day at both shelters, but you have to be a guest to take breakfast. Lunch and dinner are for anyone who's hungry."

"And the beds? Singles on the floor or bunks?"

"We mostly have bunks, but we do use some fold-away cots when we're full or for special circumstances. Rarely on both counts."

Trucks put his hand on Claudia's shoulder.

"We might be one of those," he said.

"I'm sorry, but by rule, women and children stay in the same shelter, apart from the men. For safety reasons. Men have their own shelter."

"I figured that," Trucks said. "But I can't be away from my girl. I'm sure you get that. So if we're gonna stay here, I need you to let us be a special circumstance."

The woman thought for a moment. She looked between Trucks and Claudia.

"She'll be just as safe staying in the women and children's shelter. We've got wonderful staff here all hours of the day and night and an on-call minister."

"She's safe with me. There's no exception to that. Let her stay in the men's shelter on one of the bottom bunks. Give me one of those fold-away cots. We can put it beside her. I know they're small. I know what they feel like. I've slept on them so many times I couldn't even count."

"These are set rules, sir. I'd love to help if I could."

Trucks smoothed Claudia's hair, revealing her hearing aids. Then he pulled her against him. "We don't wanna be out in the cold again tonight," he said.

Trucks squeezed Claudia. She made a pathetic face.

The woman thought hard. Then she stood.

"I'll go talk to my manager and see what we can do."

"Thank you so much. It's all I'm asking."

A few minutes later the woman came back with some paperwork.

"You'll have to sign some extra forms," she said.

"All right."

"Please put the bag on the counter. I need to go through it, check it in, and keep it in holding if you're staying the night."

Trucks lifted the duffel bag and set it on the counter. The woman unzipped every pocket. She went through the bag, sifting the food and toiletries.

"I don't see any weapons in here. Now, please answer honestly: are you carrying?"

Trucks thought about his fists. How lethal they could be.

"No," he said.

"Sign this form, please."

He signed the form.

"Do you do any drugs or drink alcohol?" she asked.

"Not in a long time." Trucks looked over at Claudia. "You haven't picked up drinking, have you?"

Claudia shook her head. The woman didn't laugh.

"We're a sober shelter and offer all services by the kindly grace of God. No alcohol or drugs are allowed on the premises. If you break the rules, you get a strike. Depending on the severity of the strikes, you could be offered another or get suspended from shelter premises for a period determined by the actionable events, sometimes permanently. Please sign here."

Trucks signed.

"Breakfast is at eight, lunch at noon, and dinner at five. You can eat at either shelter. For her sake, you might want to eat at the women and children's shelter. Commingling is fine during daylight hours. Also, we provide a nondenominational chapel service at both shelters. While attendance is voluntary and not required to receive care here, we do urge all of our guests to go in, have a look and a listen, and be open to feeling the power and the presence of God. Whether or not you're a believer, you'll still have the privilege of hearing some lovely sermons and get a chance to speak with supportive and loving people."

"That's nice," Trucks said. "It sounds good. And how about the showers?"

"You'll have to take her over to the other shelter for a shower."

"I figured," Trucks said.

"We offer towels, shampoo, soap, cotton swabs." She looked Trucks over. "Razors. Looks like you haven't shaved in a while. It might be nice, relaxing, if you want to shave."

"I suppose I should," Trucks said.

The woman tied a tag to the handle of the duffel bag with *37* written on it.

"Every time you come in, we need to go through your bag to look for weapons, alcohol, drugs, and other miscellaneous things, okay?"

Trucks nodded.

"Now, do you want to check the bag in here and leave it with us, or are you taking it out with you for the day?"

"I suppose we can leave it here."

The woman handed Trucks a wooden token with *37* burned into the grain.

"This is your token to get the bag back. If you lose the token, all you have to do is supply proof that you are who you say you are by identifying key points from this form. Please fill out the rest of it as clearly as possible, write out each of your names at the bottom, and sign."

At the bottom, he wrote: *Ezzard and Pearl Kadoka.* Then he signed his false name.

ANOTHER LESSON IN NEED BORROWING

Trucks held Claudia's hand tight as they walked through the streets. He wanted to keep her close. Keep her safe in the city. Snow was everywhere. Bare tree branches shook overhead. They looked sick, all skinny and gray. Trucks and Claudia passed building after building. Their red bricks faded. Most awnings the same. A shade of green or a washed-out blue.

Swift Thrift came into view. A sign on the glass door said all items with a yellow dot were half off. Trucks had asked the woman at the shelter where he could go for secondhand clothes. The shelter had a few bargain centers at opposite ends of town, but Swift Thrift was closer. He wanted to buy Claudia a change of warmer clothes. She'd only had her pajamas since they started. They'd gotten washed at Gerald's, but Trucks wanted her to have more layers. Still, they couldn't add much to their possessions. It always had to be light. Simple. Quick. Things with no emotional attachment. Easy to get rid of if it had to be done.

Trucks opened the door. A bell dinged when they came in. It threw him off for a second. He walked Claudia over to the clothing section and found a small rack of children's clothes.

"It smells like old blankets," she said. "Like a whole

bunch of old stuff."

"Thrift stores all smell the same."

"It's weird."

"It is. Now pick out a few sweatshirts and pants."

"Anything I want?" she asked.

"Only the tags with the yellow dots," he said.

He pulled a shirt off the rack and showed her the tag.

"See how this one's got a yellow dot?"

"Yeah."

"Find ones like this. Forget about the others."

"Why?"

"The ones with the yellow dots are the special secret clothes for the day. It's like a game to see if you can find the secret ones."

"Okay."

"So look for the yellow dots."

She started sifting through T-shirts.

"Not those. Look for thick sweatshirts. Anything that's gonna keep you warm. You can't wear T-shirts in winter, you nut."

"But I like these. Feel," she said.

Trucks felt the material.

"It's nice," he said, "but we're not getting those. Try the others on down the rack."

He pointed to the long-sleeve shirts.

"Fine," she said, and walked over.

"And some pants. Look at the pants too."

"Okay."

Trucks saw an appliance and kitchenware section.

"I'm gonna head over that way." He pointed, but she

wasn't looking. "Hey," he said.

"What?"

She kept sifting.

"Look at me."

She looked over while holding the sleeves of two shirts.

"I'm going over there real quick. Don't leave this area."

Claudia nodded.

"Tell me."

"Okay. I won't leave," she said.

Trucks walked off. He spent the next few minutes going through spatulas and picking up dented metal toasters. Screwdrivers and clothespins lay on shelves with spoons and toothpicks. He looked inside ceramic teapots and held fine cheese graders, whisks, ramekins. Things he'd never use. Still. It made him think about what it would be like to have a place with Claudia. Their own space in a new town. Just them. All the bullshit a thousand miles away where it couldn't reach them anymore. Where it couldn't beat them down. A new life. A do-over.

Trucks looked at Claudia to make sure she was still browsing. She had a few T-shirts draped over her shoulder. That stubborn kid. At least she was going through the pants now.

He looked around. An older employee helped a customer at the register. The customer was buying antique soda bottles. She had half a dozen on the counter. Trucks turned away. He noticed hockey sticks hanging from pegs on a distant wall and walked over.

He ran his finger along one of the hockey sticks. The sleek finish of the wood. He found old baseball gloves, tennis balls in a shoebox, partially deflated soccer balls. There were faded cones for drills, a stack of discs, multicolored golf tees in a shot glass.

Then he saw them in the corner. Like an old leather beacon calling him home. A pair of faded boxing gloves beaten to hell. Hung by their laces. He walked over and put his face into the gloves. He inhaled. There was nothing he missed more than that smell. The musty leather. The hint of sweat. The evidence in dark residue spots all over the gloves. He reached up and took them from the peg. Felt the leather, no longer crisp. But there was still a softness to those old, withered gloves.

If someone asked, he'd probably say he could remember his first pair. It'd be a lie. He never had a first pair of boxing gloves. His first pair changed with every training session. Drawn from a community pile in a weathered box shared by several guys in that old gym back in Klakanouse. The grip molding to the hands of each man. Shifting by the day. By the night. The sweat and blood and cuts bonding them within that leather casing.

He looked at the gloves in his hands. Someone had tied the laces together so many times that the dozens of knots looked like a hive. He told himself not to start picking at them. He wanted to pick at them so bad. Like a sickness. Undo the knots and put on the gloves. Get a feel for the grip. Think about the combinations he'd throw.

But no. If he started that up again, what kind of life was he moving toward? Probably not a better one for his girl. He'd have to try to let it go. Maybe not in mind but in body. In action. He feared it would kill him. To lose the movement. The grace. His only way of being. The only way he knew how to exist in a world he didn't otherwise understand.

"Dear! Dear!" he heard someone yell. It startled him so much he dropped the gloves. He picked them up and set them on the shelf.

Trucks felt like he'd been awakened from a dream.

The elderly clerk at the register yelled across the store. She waved her hand overhead. "We have fitting rooms for that!"

Trucks looked to where she was looking. Claudia was on the floor in her underwear, her pajama bottoms next to her. She was on her side, struggling to pull on a pair of jeans.

Trucks and the clerk arrived at the same time.

"Is this your daughter?" she asked.

Trucks bent down to help Claudia out of the pants.

"Couldn't be anyone else's with moves like that," he joked.

The clerk didn't look amused. "Changing rooms are in the corner if you need them," she said. She pointed at the changing rooms for emphasis.

"Got it," Trucks said.

He helped Claudia wiggle out of the pants and back into her pajama bottoms. The clerk walked to the register. The gawkers went back to shopping.

"Well, that was something," Trucks said.

"I just wanted to try them on," Claudia said. She looked embarrassed.

"That's why most stores have a changing room. So people don't see your privates."

"I'm sorry."

"Hey. Nothing to be sorry about, Pepper Flake. You didn't know."

"I feel stupid," she said. Then she looked around to see if anyone was staring. Her face was all red.

Trucks cupped her cheek.

"Not stupid. Not," he said.

Claudia was silent. She looked at the floor.

Trucks got down on a knee.

"You're not stupid because you don't know something. It's not your fault you don't know it. Just another thing you learned now. Think of it like that. And there's a shitload I don't even know, so imagine all the things you'll learn along the way. Okay?"

"Okay," she said.

"This is all just new experiences. Us going. Learning all these things together we don't know yet. Now look up at me."

She looked up.

"Tell me, what'd you pick out?"

Claudia grabbed two pairs of jeans from the floor—the black one she'd attempted to try on and a dark blue pair. Trucks took them. She handed him two T-shirts. One was a light caramel color with a roaring cartoon lion standing on a gray rock. The other was dark purple covered in fluttering butterflies. Then she showed him a sweatshirt. It was green with a reindeer on it. A dialogue bubble appeared next to the reindeer's open mouth. It said, "I'd rather be prancing."

"It's funny," she said. "It'd be fun to prance."

"I'm sure it would."

"Can I have these?"

"I said no T-shirts."

"But I got a sweatshirt like you said. And pants."

"What are you gonna do with T-shirts in winter?"

"Put them under the long shirt."

"You don't need them."

"But I like them."

"We live off need, not want."

Claudia pouted.

"Christ," he said.

"Please?"

He looked in her eyes. They sparkled under the store lights.

"I'll think about it," he said.

Trucks slung the shirts over his shoulder, squatted down, and held the pants up to Claudia to check the size from waist to ankle.

"I did that already," she said.

"Then why'd you take your pants off in the middle of the store and try to put these on?"

"I wanted to be sure they fit good."

"Solid thinking," he said. "We can't go wasting money."

"Because we don't have it?"

"And maybe never will. At least not the way a lot of other people do. But it's not important. What matters is what's in your heart and what you do for others. That's all there really is."

Claudia thought a moment.

"But what if we 'need borrow' like we did at the other store?"

The jeans were five dollars each. The sweatshirt three dollars. The T-shirts two dollars each. She'd picked all the ones with yellow dots. Cut at 50 percent, it'd be eight-and-a-half bucks. No sales tax in Montana—one bonus Gerald had mentioned. But still. A Third of their remaining cash on clothes? Not a chance.

"You like the black or the dark blue better?"

"Hmm, black," she said, pointing to the jeans.

"Okay. And butterflies or the lion?"

"But I like them both."

"Pick one."

"I don't like decisions."

"Tough."

"Urrrrrgh."

"Come on."

"Fine. The lion."

He handed her the dark blue jeans and the butterfly T-shirt.

"Put these back where you found them."

"Fine," she said, and took the clothes back to the rack.

Trucks watched her place the T-shirt on its hanger. She clipped the jeans to a thicker hanger and sifted through the clothes. He thought he heard her humming. He stood there in a daze watching over her. Something so sweet and delicate about how she fingered the clothing like it would shatter if touched with too much force.

Trucks walked over to her. He looked around. A staff member helped an older man unravel a garden hose. The register clerk sorted hangers.

"Listen to me," he said. "Grab the butterfly shirt."

She did.

"You think it fits?"

She nodded.

"Give it to me."

She handed it over.

'Unzip your coat halfway."

She unzipped it.

"Here."

Trucks stuffed the shirt into her coat.

"Up," he said.

She zipped up her coat with a smile.

Trucks put a finger to his lips.

They walked to the counter, an intense energy between them. Trucks paid five dollars for the items. The woman placed them in a plastic bag, and they left the store.

When they got outside and the door banged shut, Claudia growled with excitement.

"A nice rush, huh?" Trucks said.

"Yeah!"

They were a half block down the street when Claudia stopped. She opened her coat and pulled out the shirt. Then she put the shirt to her face and inhaled.

"Still smells like old stuff," she said.

"It'll take a few washes in the sink to get that out," he said. "Now tuck it away before you get us busted."

Claudia put the shirt inside her coat and zipped it up.

"So what's that called?" she asked. "What we did just now."

"Another version of need borrowing, I guess," he said.

"So there are more kinds of it?"

"Sure. Nothing's just black and white, Pepper Flake. Everything's gray in the world, except that you'll live and you'll die. There's no gray in that. It's certain."

Claudia looked distressed.

"Hey, don't worry about it. We've got so much time left you couldn't even count it all if you wanted to."

CATCHING THE GHOST

The first night in the shelter was all right. The blankets were stiff and scratchy. The same feel he'd remembered from all his times taking Claudia to shelters before he and Elle landed that dive row house near the tracks. He was thankful Claudia didn't remember.

Trucks didn't sleep. He lay in the small cot beside Claudia and watched her rest. He suddenly felt he'd lost control. It was strange, considering they were safe, fed, and had a place to stay. He was grateful for it. No matter how uncomfortable it made him to be there, he was grateful. But being in a shelter wasn't the life he'd intended. He lay there thinking of it. Constantly scanning the room for movement. He was always defensive, so being in a shelter with dozens of strangers didn't do his stress any good. Having his girl there only made it worse. Heightened his fight instincts. His protective nature.

Trucks put his hands behind his head and looked up. After enough time in the darkness he could see. The staff had left a few nightlights on, but one of the homeless men had shut them off or plucked them out of the sockets soon after lights out.

There was a slight hum in the room. Trucks looked over at Claudia. She was on her side in the lower bunk. He had her sleep against the close edge so he could see her. He was lower than her on the cot, so he could only look at that angle.

No. This wasn't the life he'd imagined when he decided he'd take his girl back. The thought was more idealistic than this. The two of them hitching all those miles. Meeting strangers with interesting stories and lives. Showing his girl parts of the country she'd never seen. He'd accomplished some of it. But being in Billings, sleeping in the shelter, felt static. Like their lives were frozen. Maybe that's why he loved boxing so much, the constant movement. Up on the toes. Throw when there's an opening, shift the position, always on the hunt or the run. It was the only way he knew how to live. It was the way he liked to live. He was trying to figure out how to bring this to his girl. How to bring that to the life they were leading now. He didn't know how to do it without boxing. But he could try. Wasn't this trying?

For no reason, he thought about the ghost of Holly Jack Rose. Wondered where he was now. If he was still slipping punches out in Detroit like a slick apparition. A flicker of movement. There and gone. *Poof.* Trucks had always wondered how he'd worked his feet in that way. Was mesmerized by the movement. Sometimes he wondered if he'd ever really clipped Holly Jack Rose. Or was it a wishful memory? Something he'd created and tucked away to make him feel like he'd caught the ghost so maybe he could put it to bed in his own way.

Trucks rubbed his eyes. He put his hands on his stomach. The free clinic had introduced him to a naturopath once who told him to use the power in his hands to transfer the energy between his organs and palms. Whatever the hell that meant. Sure, he knew how to displace energy. He'd done it all his life. Had trained in the art of bringing it up from the legs and the hips. Putting it all into the torque of the body. The output of punishment from his fists like quick-pap lightning strikes. A therapist at the same free clinic had told him years ago that she wished he'd use that violent energy in some other way. He'd asked, like what? She'd said, like to love yourself. The concept had never occurred to him. But it bothered him for years after.

He thought now about what it meant to love himself. He'd been left by his parents. Known surrogates at children's homes all his life. Nothing real. Nothing blood. His family was in the gym. It's what he made it into, anyway. Though he didn't know if he could say he loved any of the people he'd met there. And had he really loved Elle? Or was it merely the sickness? Caused by that chemical reaction of the two of them together that made him burn inside when she was close. Had he just been clinging to a person he'd wanted to show him love but never truly did? Did it happen that way because it was all he knew? Was it just something he'd made? He never knew who or what to blame. Always himself, in the end. Probably the best answer. And he often lay awake at night wondering how a person like him could ever love himself. How sick someone else would have to be to love him back.

But there was always Claudia. A happy mistake. He'd put all the energy he had left—between putting in rounds at the gym and taking fights—into her and her life. But had it been enough? Would it ever be?

Without realizing it, he was rotating fist over fist. Staring at the ceiling. All those learned responses to tension. Things he never thought of. Things he just did on instinct. Like the going. The going was what he knew. What he craved. What his body told him to do when it pulled at him in the night.

Trucks looked over at Claudia. He reached out and put his hand on her. He felt her pulsing warmth against his palm. He closed his eyes and listened to the hum of the room.

NONPEOPLE

In the morning he checked the opportunities board posted in the shelter lobby. Several jobs and cleanup programs were listed. He was thankful he wasn't an addict. At least with substances. A lot of the jobs required a high school diploma, which he didn't have.

Claudia tugged on his coat sleeve.

"Hang on a minute," he said.

"I'm hungry," she said.

"Soon. I promise," he said.

She let go and leaned against the wall, pulled the copper gambling token from her pocket.

Trucks looked over the board and the city map. He'd have to walk her around town and see if there were any openings at the universities and community centers. The board became a blur. It wasn't his kind of thing, looking for regular jobs like this. He'd relied so long on his fists, his instincts, taking that smooth stride across the ring. This felt stiff. False. Like he was living in someone else's body. But he was doing it for her. Everything for his girl. He had to keep telling himself that. He must.

After breakfast they got to walking.

"It's gonna take a couple hours," he said.

"Okay," she said.

"We're looking for a new job for me," he said. "It's not boxing. I'm not boxing," he said, more to himself than her.

"I don't wanna see you all hurt anymore," she said. "It's just real bad."

They walked through the cold and the gray. Past lots of people who seemed to brighten when they saw the two of them. Always something about a man and his girl.

They stopped at the community center to check the main desk and bulletin boards for job openings. The community center had little to offer, mostly a place for retirees and senior citizens to gather and play cards, have donuts and coffee, talk about the past they all missed. Claudia had spotted an older guy in a maroon sweater with a bowler hat and thought it was Gerald. It wasn't. But it made Trucks wonder where her mind was.

They headed northwest and walked around the Montana State University satellite campus. Claudia got a lot of smiles from girls rushing between classes with books in their arms. Backpacks weighing them down. It made Trucks feel old. Out of place. He realized he'd never been on a college campus before. It didn't feel impressive. The buildings red stone and boxy and generic.

Then they came across a full-size horse statue. It stared dead-eyed over the sidewalk.

"I wanna get on," Claudia said. "Can I get on?"

Trucks looked around. He pulled out his sachet of antibacterial wipes and scrubbed down the horse. Then he boosted her up.

"Brrrrr, it's cold on my butt!" she said.

Trucks laughed. He looked around again. The students

were walking and chatting. Paying them no mind.

Claudia put her hands at the sides of the horse's thick neck. She looked into its mane like a crystal ball. Trucks walked around and stood in front of the horse. He stared into its intense, dark eyes.

"So where we going?" Trucks asked.

"Riding to the water," Claudia said. "*Bup-a, bup-a, bup-a, bup.*"

The sounds took Trucks back to his days learning the speed bag. Just a young kid floating the streets. Didn't know anyone. Didn't trust anyone. Didn't have a friend to talk the day away. Instead he listened to the trainers and the older kids. Put a wooden box on the floor of that old gym and stepped up. Faced the speed bag. Took him weeks to find the rhythm. To hit the bag more than a few consecutive times without messing up. But once he got it, learned how to catch the speed bag with the outer edge of the fist, it was like he had a new friend. He'd work both hands. Go for a while with the right, switch to the left. Go intermittent with both. And once he had it down and that speed bag was blurring, he'd close his eyes and listen to its fast bang against the upper board. The sweet swing of the short chain. Fist on resin. And it'd speak to him. Go: *Bop-a-dup, bop-a-dup, bop-a-dup, bop-a-dup.* And when he was down and lonely and hurt, thinking of how his mother and father had taken off, dumped him under the eaves of a children's home, which lead to home after home after nobody-gives-a-fuck-about-you home, he'd run to the gym. He'd breathe hard and wrap his hands. Step up on that wooden box and talk to his only friend: *Bop-a-dup, bop-a-dup, bop-a-dup, bop-a-dup.*

The push and swing. The power of those small fists and what they could make in the world. What they could break.

And he heard again now: "*Bup-a, bup-a, bup-a, bup.*" And it brought him back.

"Where…where to the water?" Trucks asked.

"Where there's no sharks," Claudia said. "I don't wanna get bit."

"I don't blame you," he said.

"It'd hurt real bad. You'd die," she said.

"You would," he said. "Probably."

Claudia sat up straight. She put her big-gloved hands on her knees.

"People survive big attacks like that sometimes," Trucks said.

"How?"

"I don't know. Pure luck. Can't be anything more. A big beast like that. All those huge, jagged teeth. I can't imagine."

"Yuck."

"Yeah. But they're pretty sleek how they move. Just got that one vicious goal: go forward and attack."

Claudia shook her head. "Come get me down," she said.

Trucks stared again into the eyes of the horse. Built sturdy and thick. More muscular than any horse he'd ever seen. How fast it could go. How far it could carry them if it was more than fixed stone.

Trucks walked around to the side and got Claudia down. She adjusted her hood and pointed to her ear.

"Can you fix it?" she asked.

"What's wrong?"

"I hit the button on my hearing phone."

Trucks didn't correct her. He bent down and pulled her hood back, checked both her hearing aids. The volume dial on the right side had been turned down. He rolled it up to where she liked it.

"Good?" he asked.

She gave him a thumbs-up. He pulled her hood forward.

"We gotta keep going. We'll stay warmer that way," he said.

As they crossed the snow-lined campus, he reached over and rubbed her back.

Soon they found the student union and checked the opportunities boards. Most of the postings were unrelated to work—ads for roommates, tutors, carpooling, study groups. The few listed positions were strictly for students or jobs he wasn't qualified for. One of the guys at the shelter had mentioned jobs were scarce but that the university sometimes had openings for janitorial staff or maintenance crew. But Trucks saw nothing like that. No possibilities at all.

Trucks took them by the stone horse again so Claudia could have another ride. He didn't dare look the stone horse in the eyes this time. Like it might show disappointment. Blame him for it all.

They cut across the campus and continued west. Little traffic zipped by. A plane took off from the airport just north of them. Claudia stopped and watched in awe, a hand over her eyes. She followed the plane until it went through the clouds and out of sight. The vapor trail it left behind as a reminder of where it'd been.

Then they turned and walked on.

After a few miles they reached the Rocky Mountain College campus. It was more of what Trucks imagined about a university. Gray stone buildings with angular roofs. Quiet. Peaceful. They walked into the student center, and he searched the boards. Still, nothing. Not a single opening that would work.

Trucks tapped Claudia's shoulder, and they tightened their coats and walked out.

They were quiet on the long walk back. Trucks felt like he was betraying the heart of himself by looking for common jobs. Instead of returning to the shelter, he took her to a diner and bought her a couple donuts. He didn't know what else to do.

IN THE SMALL HOURS

The night had come again. Lights out. Bulbs taken.

Trucks listened to the hum of the room. Could almost feel it within him. The slight vibrations. The little withdrawals from trying to let go of such a vast part of himself.

He looked over at his girl. She was asleep with her mouth slightly open. Taking the big breaths of youth. He reached over and touched her soft elbow with his fingertips. He left them there a few seconds before pulling his hand back.

He was trying to give her a new life and a new way. To leave the boxing behind in favor of whatever else might come. Hopefully something without pain and punishment and blood loss. But weren't those things that had made him what he was? Built the armor that he'd used to protect his girl and the life they'd forged together? She reacted to his boxing like it was a sin to throw a punch, to take one, to set a single foot on the hallowed canvas. But what did she know of what it had given them? What did she know of what it had taken away?

These were the things that plagued him in the small hours. All these nameless bodies lying around him in a mortuary of sleep. The only one that mattered a few feet away. How he'd watch and watch and watch, until finally he drifted off too. His thoughts a blur of questions. His love hung on the movements of her hummingbird breaths.

THE DYNAMOS

The next morning Trucks noticed a posting for the Billings Public Library. A page position shelving books. He
thought back to the night before. How if he was going to
kick this thing and start a life without boxing, he'd have to
go as far away from it as possible. The library was prom-
ising in that way. Even though a high school diploma was
required, he could lie. They probably wouldn't even check.

Trucks looked around, then he tore the ad off the board.
He folded it up and put it in his back pocket. Claudia was
on the ground now, trying to arch her back as high as possible.

"You gonna be a gymnast dynamo or something?" he
asked.

"I don't know. Maybe. What's that?"

"Someone who's really good at something. Like they've
got a born knack for it that others don't."

"Hmm. Could I be one?" Claudia asked when she sat up.

"I don't know. As you grow, we'll figure out what you're
great at."

"You think I'll be great at something?"

"Definitely."

He held out his hand. She took it, and he pulled her up.
Then he buttoned the throat flaps on her coat before they

headed out.

"What about you?" she asked.

"What about me?" He watched the traffic before they crossed the street.

"Are you a diamond-mo?"

"Dynamo."

"Dime-uh-mo?"

"Think of it like dinosaur. You can say that."

"Dinosaur."

"Good, now take out *saur* and add *mo*."

"Dyna...mo," she said. "Dynamo."

"Good, see? You're a fast learner, Pepper Flake."

"Cause of you," she said.

"You want some food, we better get moving," he said, and pulled her into the street. "Come on! Run, little legs."

They laughed as they ran across the street on their way to breakfast.

THE BILLINGS PUBLIC LIBRARY

The library looked like a giant glass box. Beautiful. Surrounded in hundreds of windows. A view of the mountains lining the background. Trucks and Claudia had gawked at the oval ceiling hole in the center of the main floor. It reminded him of an eggshell stripped thin. Painted in its own yolk. Claudia said they were in a spaceship. He'd asked where it would take them. She'd just pointed at the ceiling and said, "Up."

Trucks and Claudia sat on a black couch under the oval as he filled out an application for the page position. Under work history, he didn't put down that he'd boxed to earn a living. Instead he wrote the name of the gym where he'd trained. To save money on dues, he'd spent a lot of late nights mopping the mats, wiping down the benches and weights, putting away the headgear and gloves and wraps, sweeping the ring. He figured he could put that down.

"You enjoying those?" he asked Claudia.

She flipped through some kids' magazines he'd nabbed when they first got there.

"Bored," she said.

"I'm working on something for us," he said.

She smiled like it was a secret he'd surprise her with.

"A good job possibility. I might get this one, you never

know."

The application was only a page. Trucks put down KHS under education, though he'd never finished high school. He'd spent a few years at Klakanouse High School, probably worked his way up to a sophomore in completed credits. He couldn't remember. It didn't really matter. He'd lie about it and see. Who was really going to call a high school over a minimum-wage job?

Trucks completed the form. He told Claudia to sit tight and walked to the main desk. He handed the paper to the librarian who'd given him the form. She quickly scanned his application, then said, "Your contact number, it's from the rescue mission, is that right?"

"That's right," he said.

"I wanted to be sure. You put *Beartooth* after the number."

"I figured I should write that so if you call you'll know to ask them to find me. I might not be there. It depends. I'll be in and out quite a bit with my girl." He pointed at Claudia. She'd rolled up one of the magazines like a telescope and was watching them.

"That's adorable," the librarian said.

"She's something," Trucks said.

"From your application, it looks like you don't have any experience in the field."

"I don't."

"Well, it's not a requirement for the job. We've hired many people over the years who have no experience. These days, it's just a nice bonus when someone's familiar with the stacks."

Trucks didn't know what she meant by *stacks*. He thought

of all the wins he'd pulled off in a row early in his career without a single loss. People would say he was "stacking them up." His wins like knocked-out bodies on the ground in stacks. Or the smokestacks on the outskirts of Klakanouse where he'd lived in a children's home when he was eight. He remembered running laps around the home to build his wind, watching the black smoke float through the sky.

"It's mostly just sorting the books from the return bins, separating them on carts by section—children's, fiction, nonfiction, magazines—then sorting them by genre or Dewey number, depending. After that you would shelve the books. It's not too hard once you get started. Have you done any shelving?"

Trucks didn't know what a Dewey number was. But the job didn't sound so hard. Maybe boring but not difficult.

"Not exactly, no," he said. "I've hung up a lot of equipment back at the gym. Put pads and gloves and bags and mats on shelves and hooks. It's kinda similar."

The librarian nodded. "That's good," she said.

The librarian set another form on the desk. Four stapled pages, front-to-back print.

"What's that?" Trucks asked.

"It's our customary sorting and logical deduction aptitude test. Everyone who applies must take it. I know, it's kind of a bother, but it shouldn't take more than twenty minutes. Some fill-in-the-blank questions, some multiple choice. Don't worry about it. I'm sure you'll do fine."

Trucks grabbed the form.

"Thanks. Good thing I've got my girl with me, she'll know all the answers," he joked.

The librarian gave an uncomfortable laugh.

Trucks thanked her again and walked back to Claudia. He sat next to her and put the test on the circular wooden table.

"Can we go now?" she asked.

"Just about. I just need to fill out some more papers."

"Again?"

"Yeah."

"What are we doing after?"

"I don't know, Pepper Flake. Just give me a little time to get this done, okay?"

Trucks rested his elbows on his knees. He covered his face with his hands, closed his eyes, and sighed hard. He wasn't much of a test taker. From what he'd seen of the questions, he didn't have a damn clue. So he did what he always did and gave it a shot. He took the pen and worked through the problems. Questions about numbers before and after decimals, how to arrange books if *Mc* and *Mac* and *Maac* are on the same cart. What was meant by the abbreviations YA, F, NF, AF, CB, TP, and on and on. Some things he could work out. Some he couldn't. Whenever he'd get stuck, Trucks would look over at Claudia. He'd feel real warm inside as he watched her trying to make houses out of the magazines. Roll them up, one in each hand, and tap the edge of the table like a drum kit.

Trucks walked the finished test up to the librarian. He handed it to her. She skimmed it with a finger. Looked up at him.

"We'll let you know," she said. "Calls will probably go out within the week. We notify all applicants, either way."

"I don't know a lot about the books, but I work hard. I've done some shelving, like I said."

"It sounds like it," she said.

"I know it's not your kind of shelving, but it was real work. I arranged things."

Trucks opened and closed his bad hand by his hip.

"We haven't had too many applicants yet. Really, as long as you passed the test and your history seems like a fit, I'm sure you'll get a call with some good news."

"I'd really appreciate it. I just want you to know that. I'd do good."

"I don't doubt it," the librarian said. Then she took off her glasses. "I'm really not the one hiring, so I won't have an impact on your application or your chances."

Trucks looked over at Claudia. He tapped his knuckles against his leg.

"Okay. Well, maybe you could pass it along. Let them know the guy who did the application works hard. And he's…he's a good guy. He'd be happy to shelve or do cleaning or whatever needs to be done."

"Will do. I better get back to it here," she said.

"Sure," Trucks said. "Thanks for the time."

"Good luck, um…" The librarian looked through the papers. "Mr. Kadoka. I'm sure you'll be hearing from us."

Trucks squeezed his fist tight. He turned and walked over to Claudia.

"Okay, Pepper Flake, we gotta put these magazines back," he said.

Then he walked Claudia over to the children's section, and she put the magazines back.

Before they walked out, they stood next to the entrance and put on their coats. Trucks made sure her hood was tight. He buttoned her throat flaps. Claudia reached inside the hood and adjusted her hearing aids. She stared up at him when she was ready.

When the librarian looked over, Trucks gave her a wave. She waved back. Then Trucks walked his girl out the door and into the biting Montana winter.

He didn't say anything as they walked along, but he felt a warmth inside. Like the rare feeling of hope. Claudia moved in a light skip. Trucks listened to her sing under her breath. He thought about how happy she seemed in the library. Its unique chairs and colored lights. The angled architecture. Thousands of square feet of pristine carpet. Everything tight and crisp and clean and in its place. The shelves making homes for worlds they might finally know.

NIGHT BREATH

Trucks lay awake in the cot, trying hard not to smell. One of the homeless guys had vomited all over the floor just before lights out. Even though the staff had cleaned it up, the smell hung heavy.

Trucks was feeling hopeful about the job. He'd never felt this way about something so apart from his known world. The hope made him sick. Trucks put his hands on his stomach. He didn't know how to displace his energy from his hands to his organs. But he thought about it again. Tried to remember what the naturopath had said back when he and his trainer were trying to get his body right. So many years of boxing takes its toll. The stress and anxiety of attack and defend, attack and defend, did no good for him. At least not in the real world. Not in any practical way. Sure, it won him fights. It put him in a good headspace for the ring world but not for the working world. Or the world where he was trying to raise his girl. Teach her morals as he knew them. The ways to treat others. How to treat herself.

He'd never taught her to box. Part of him was never sure if it was a good idea. Elle had so much intensity and heat to her, he feared it would come out in Claudia too. And maybe the boxing would only make it worse. Bring it out faster. Force her to snap so much sooner than she might anyway.

Or maybe snapping wasn't part of her makeup. Maybe it would skip her blood. He hoped for that. That his little girl wouldn't be anything like Elle when she got older. That maybe all they'd have in common were those long, dark curls. A beautiful thing.

Trucks turned on his side. He kept his coat on the ground near the bed. He dug in a pocket and pulled out his sachet. Trucks opened the sachet and waited for that familiar smell to rise. A draft of gardenias. Those dangerous things. He put his busted hands together and closed his eyes. He put all the energy he had into trying to see Elle again in that bar all those years ago. Back when he first met her. When it felt like the spark of him and her meant something good. When it radiated between them like a tension of love and understanding and what could be. But it was too hard to picture anything like that now. All he ever imagined was her cold body in a ditch. Her skin so pale and blue in the darkness. It had been years since he'd seen her or heard from her, so there was little else to suspect. She'd become the kind of woman who woke up with the needle still stuck in her arm. The syringe lying at an angle from tossing in her sleep. The knot still tied off. Blood trickling from the entry point. It's not how he wanted to think of her. Dead isn't how he wanted to see her. But he couldn't control what his mind showed him. And be it sickness or love, the fact that he still thought of her kept her alive in the spirit of the world. Because at least someone was thinking of her. That poor soul.

Suddenly he was aware of the hum in the room again. A noise that came with the night. He blinked and looked into the darkness. Wondered if there was anyone out there thinking of him. And if he died, who would be there to mourn him? Who would care enough to keep him alive in their memory?

He looked over at Claudia. She was asleep on her side. Her lips shook when she breathed in that way. He liked how heavy it was. Like she was letting him know she was still alive. That her wind was good and strong in those little lungs.

Trucks got up on his elbow. He looked around the room. There wasn't much he could see. The nightlights were gone again. He wondered if the homeless men took them out of the wall sockets. Put the bulbs in bed against their skin under the sheets to take in the warmth of the cooling glass.

He kissed his thumb and ran it over Claudia's eyebrow. She twitched but didn't wake. He brought his hand back and cracked his knuckles under the sheets. He thought of how he always did that before putting on the boxing gloves. And after taking them off. How he'd shake out his hands to release the tightness, to open up the blood. Feel his wrists slip into place. The crack of the bones.

She was too delicate for it. He knew he should never teach her. But a good part of him wanted to pass something on, and wasn't that the only real trade he had? The evidence of a depth of knowledge he'd gained over all his years? So he couldn't tell her about Dewey numbers or how to grow vegetables or calculate prescriptions or what happens in the stock market. But he could teach her how to throw a right cross, slip a punch, step away from the power, slide into the pocket.

It was too much to think about now. The hanging smell

of vomit gave him a headache. He reached over and put his hand on Claudia. He'd leave it there until his arm fell asleep or she woke and turned. Trucks closed his eyes and pulled the scratchy blanket over his nose. He breathed into the material, and the warmth of his breath returned to him, like the blanket was breathing right back.

EVERYTHING'S ALL RIGHT, ISN'T IT?

Trucks and Claudia sat in the shelter lobby for hours. He was waiting for a phone call from the library. He didn't figure it would come that morning, but he was hopeful it might. They'd had breakfast when the doors opened, then came straight back. Claudia had been so composed and patient. He really admired her for that. For putting up with him and all that he asked of her.

He reached out and squeezed her knee.

"You wanna get moving?" he asked.

"Yeah, a lot," she said.

"Hang tight, then."

Trucks stood and walked to the counter. He handed over the wooden token with *37* burned into it. The woman went to the back where there were rows of cubbies and returned with the navy duffel bag. Trucks pulled out a plastic bag from the side pocket. He filled it with a jar of peanut butter, a knife, a few apples, some crackers, and bottles of water. Then he gave the duffel bag back. He asked the woman several questions. She gestured, gave directions, and signaled where to go. Trucks thanked her and walked over to Claudia.

"Let's hit it," he said.

Claudia jumped up. They zipped and buttoned their coats and headed for the door. Trucks paused and looked back one more time. He imagined hard that the phone would ring. They'd ask for him. He'd get on the line with the hiring manager who'd tell him he was a perfect fit. Just the guy they were looking for. He'd accept the job and hang up and hug his girl so tight. He could hardly imagine a job so peaceful. The building like a church. Calm. Quiet. Still. Something light-years from what he'd known. An opportunity that could really change things. Bring in decent pay. Safety. A new start. That fresh thing he'd been telling his girl about.

Claudia tugged on his sleeve. Trucks snapped out of it and turned.

They walked through the door. The stinging wind was back. Trucks looked down to make sure Claudia's coat was cinched up. He was taking her to the northeastern edge of town, so at least they'd have their backs to the wind on the way.

"Where we going?" she asked.

"You'll see. It's nothing special, but it should be nice."

Claudia looked confused.

"You wanna guess?" he asked.

"No."

"Why not?"

"Let's keep it for a surprise," she said.

"Okay, but it's really not a big deal. You'll probably be more disappointed than surprised," he said.

As they walked, Claudia took June's perfume out of her pocket. She pulled off one of her gloves, tucked it between her elbow and ribs, dabbed some of the perfume on her finger, and rubbed it on both sides of her neck. Then she

capped the little shampoo bottle and returned it to her pocket. Trucks could smell June real heavy in the air.

"You love that stuff," he said.

"Yeah. I miss her," Claudia said.

"You think about her a lot?"

"I don't know. Sometimes she's in my dreams. And those
are usually pretty good ones. Except when she gets far away
and disappears. Or when we're waiting on the road hitching
and she doesn't stop. Like she's mad at us now."

"Do you think she's mad at us?"

"We were all friends and had fun. Then we left her. She
was really nice to us, but she didn't have to be. She did nice
things that other people don't."

Trucks patted her hood.

"I know what you mean," he said.

"I don't know why we had to leave."

"It's not easy to explain. I tried to explain after you had
your bath in the hotel. Maybe I didn't do a good job of it."

"Why do we have to leave people who give us stuff and
be nice? Aren't we looking for them? I thought that's why we
always go. Cause we wanted to find the good."

Trucks thought as they walked along. The sack of supplies brushed against his leg with each step. Traffic was slow-
er than he'd imagined. People who passed would smile and
nod. He'd expected a bigger-city feel. More hostility. He just
didn't know anything about Montana or its cities or way of
life. He could only go on his expectations and what Gerald
had said. So far, Gerald was right. The people seemed mostly
kind and giving. Trucks knew he needed to let go of expectations founded on nothing but assumption.

"Don't we want the good?" she asked.

"Of course," he said.

"So why do we leave it?"

"I don't know. It's hard to explain. Hey, are you feeling warm enough? Doing okay?"

"I'm okay," she said.

"Okay."

They walked in silence for a bit.

"We want the good, but sometimes we have to leave it behind because the good comes with other things. Things you've already felt now as a kid and will only feel stronger when you grow up."

"Like what?"

"Like expectations. Like disappointment. Like people come into your life and start out real good, and you think you've really found something. You draw this picture in your head of what you think they are. What they maybe make themselves out to be. Then, after a while—sometimes it's weeks, sometimes months, sometimes years—their *real* self comes out. Sometimes it's only kinda bad. Sometimes it's real bad. And sometimes it's so awful you can't stand to look at it because maybe what you see in the deepest dark parts of them are your own sicknesses. The hidden places inside you that nobody else gets to see. The things you have to live with because you're you. And maybe you were born with it, like a knock in the head, or maybe it's something that came about because you were dropped from shelter to shelter and home to home until you didn't even know who you were anymore. Just passed around like an unwanted gift. The kind of thing nobody wants but everyone takes for a while. I don't know,

Pepper Flake. This is hard stuff. Maybe I shouldn't be saying this."

He looked over at her as they walked. Her face was calm.

"It's okay," she said. "I wanna know. 'Cause what if you go too? If you're gone like them, then I wanna know everything. I wanna know before you leave."

Trucks reached out and held her hand.

"What do you mean? I'm not going anywhere. I've told you so many times."

"But when we were hitching you said you were gray 'cause of the camera."

"The what?"

She thought a moment. "You said you were gray 'cause of the good and bad people make. The camera."

"Oh. You mean karma."

"Yeah. You said I'm one of the good ones, but if you can turn gray, then what if I turn gray? And what if you see my dark spots and get scared and wanna go?"

"It's not gonna happen. You're the only person who gives meaning to what I do. And I'm such a fuck-up that, if anything, you'd wanna leave me, not the other way around."

"No! I wouldn't," she said. She pulled her hand away.

"We're doing our best. I know that much," he said. "My whole life all I've tried to do is protect you. That's my job. To give all I can and make sure no harm comes to you. Whatever it takes is what it takes. And maybe I've not done so good sometimes, but I've put a lot into it, and I think that counts for something. But what you really wanna know is why we left June. And I kinda covered that already. It's about not owing anyone. About being careful of the people who seem to have too much good and too much light. And maybe she really was as wonderful as she seemed. I don't know. I can't see beyond the obvious signals sometimes. But just know we didn't leave her because she seemed to have bad. We left because she seemed to have *no* bad, and that can be scarier than the other sometimes. Because you can imagine the kind of hope that builds inside, and what would that do to a person if that hope was broken? I don't wanna know. But anyway, does that help? Isn't that what you wanted to know?"

Claudia nodded. Then she said, "And to know about Mama."

"I promised I'd tell you when the time was right. It's a hard thing to talk about. It won't make you feel good. It'll be difficult. It's really just something for when you're older and can maybe handle it better. And I swear on everything that I'll tell you when it's right. I hope you trust that."

Claudia didn't say anything.

"Do you trust that?"

"I don't know."

"I need you to trust me. I've gotten us this far, right?"

"Yeah."

"So trust me. You're safe. I'm not dead. We've got food and a place to stay. Everything's all right, isn't it?"

Claudia nodded.

"We're making it in the world, aren't we?"

She nodded again.

"So have some faith in me."

"What's faith?"

Trucks laughed. "When you believe in something you have no solid reason to believe in."

They walked in silence the rest of the way. Trucks using his memory to call up the directions the woman had given him. They angled down the streets. Sometimes stopping in alleys to look at hand-drawn posters for music gigs or art galleries.

When they finally got to the place, Trucks stopped and looked up. Claudia did the same. Nuts and bolts and all kinds of microchips and wires were painted in a scatter across the awning. Trucks reached for the door handle. It looked like Gadget Ratchet was open for business.

GADGET RATCHET

The store was the size of a large closet. The man behind the counter worked on Claudia's left hearing aid. The one that had been giving her trouble from the start. She sat in a plastic chair against the wall and held the other hearing aid in her hand. Trucks had suggested she take it out to keep from throwing off the balance in her head. Though he didn't know anything about wearing a hearing aid. He just figured.

Trucks leaned against the wall. The protective outer shell of the hearing aid was flipped over on the counter. He watched the man switch from working a mini-screwdriver to picking at the guts of the hearing aid with a small tweezers. Trucks couldn't believe how complicated the inside was. All the tiny moving parts. The processor chip and amplifier and receiver. The man cut and stripped the ends to a skinny new wire. He pulled out the old wire and replaced it with the slick new one. The whole time his glasses were sliding down his nose. He had his tongue between his teeth. He concentrated that way. It reminded Trucks of some of the odd quirks he'd seen in fellow boxers. The twitch of an eyelid. Cocking the head slightly to one side or the other. Rotating the glove in and back when waiting to launch.

"Getting close now," the man said. But he never looked up. Like he was just egging himself on.

Trucks looked down at Claudia. She had on her new black jeans and green sweatshirt from the thrift store. The one with the reindeer. She traced the good hearing aid in her hand with a fingernail. He thought he heard her making little sounds like she was fixing the hearing aid. Just like the man.

On the counter, down from the man, was an old sewing machine. Its casing was off and resting on its side. He could see the pulley and bobbin case and connecting rods. The arm and bed shafts dismantled. Next to it was a radio. Beside that a beige vacuum. On the small shelves, just over the shoulder of the leaning man, were scattered screwdrivers, needles, wires, pliers, folded rags. Probably about anything a man would need to work the trade. Then something entirely out of place. Right in the middle of the repairing fray. A ceramic gentleman from decades ago. Hair chestnut brown. A matching moustache. A baby blue tuxedo coat and matching pants. Black shoes. White gloves. Bowtie too square. A violet boutonniere. One arm dangling straight, the other at his waist and edge of his suit jacket like he was in the middle of reaching for a hidden gun. He had an expression. An open mouth. A look of sadness and fear in his eyes. Like he was confronting something out of his control. Like this movement would change the rest of his life.

Trucks heard a light snap.

"That's about it," the man said. He held the hearing aid up to the light and flipped it around. He did it like he was holding an emerald.

"That fast, huh?" Trucks said. He took a few steps to the counter.

"Doesn't take much. Had a loose wire. The amp was a little distorted too. With some fidgeting and fixing, I think I got it about right."

The man handed the hearing aid to Trucks. Trucks held it in his palm and raised and lowered his hand. Feeling the weight of it. It meant nothing about whether or not the fixes had worked. He just had that sad ceramic figure on his mind.

"We'll need to get the little one over here to test it out. Let us know how she's hearing with it. I usually get the bigger hearing aids to work on. People from the old folks' home on Parkhill. Bigger ears with age seems to be a truth."

The man waved Claudia over. She jumped out of the plastic chair and came up to the counter. Trucks hooked the fixed hearing aid over her left ear and fit in the earmold. Then he grabbed the other one and did the same. He turned on both hearing aids, heard and felt the clicks. Then he rolled the dials to where she usually heard best.

The man leaned on his elbows and looked over the counter.

"Hey there," Trucks said to Claudia. "You hearing everything okay?"

"Yup," she said, and gave the man a thumbs-up. "It's not blurry anymore. You fixed my hearing phones."

The man laughed. "Well, if your 'hearing phones' ever need fixing again, you can stop on by."

"Get your coat on and grab our sack," Trucks said to Claudia. Then he turned to the man. "I guess we need to settle up. We came from the Beartooth Rescue Mission. The woman at the desk said you give deals to people in hardship. She said you probably still did, anyway. That true?"

The man looked at Claudia. She had her coat on and was

getting into the oversized gloves.

"Sure thing. For the kid. For the hardship. Let's just say five bucks. In the future, you need any fixes, just promise to come back again or tell others about us, okay?"

Trucks agreed. He pulled the folded wad of cash from his pocket and peeled off five ones. He laid them on the counter. Then he stuck out his hand, and the man shook it.

"I'm grateful," Trucks said. "If my girl can hear clear again, that puts us in a better place."

"Agreed," the man said. "Remember to stop on back. And tell anyone who needs something electronic fixed, I'm the guy. Big or small, weird or not. Don't matter to me any."

"Will do," Trucks said.

The man turned from them and onto his next project.

Trucks reached for Claudia's throat flaps. Snapping them together had become reflexive. He held the door for her as she walked out ahead of him carrying their sack of supplies. Then he looked back one more time. The man was bent over the cracked-open sewing machine. Working his hands in its metal guts. Humming a calm tune. Trucks had to take another look at the porcelain statue. Something about it unnerved him, but he couldn't place what. And something about the violet boutonniere, from this distance and angle and the light coming in from the door, didn't look like a simple, delicate flower. It looked like the bleeding spread of a fatal wound.

TWO MOON PARK

They walked east. Away from Empire Steel and Iron Works and a few machine and welding shops. They took a little road along the Yellowstone River. Cut past the water plant. When the road ran out, they kept going. It was a long walk. They went several miles, but Claudia didn't complain. The river was frozen over, but Trucks led her up to it anyway. They stood at the riverbank and looked down at the ice-hardened water. The sun long gone behind a thicket of clouds. The world gray again.

"Well, it's maybe not much to see now," Trucks said. "But I wanted you to have a look."

"Were fish in there?" Claudia asked.

"Still are."

"How?"

"I don't know. Maybe they're more made for the cold."

"But it's frozen," she said, pointing at the ice. "Why aren't they dead?"

"They probably know where the warm pockets are deep down. Between rocks. Probably swim to the bottom where it's warmer. Stay away from the ice surface."

"Is that what you'd do if you were a fish?" she asked.

"Probably. Except I'd grab you first and bring you down with me. We'd find some algae to eat and have a nice winter."

"And if we were fish, we wouldn't have to hitch. We could just drive ourselves through the water."

Trucks laughed. "I suppose."

"Yeah," she said. "Do you think it'd be fun if we lived down there as fish?"

"I don't know that the lives of fish are all that fun. I imagine it's pretty dark and cold, and you'd be having to dodge enemy fish and watch out for fishing hooks and snakes and bears trying to pick you outta the water."

"That sounds scary," she said.

He realized he wasn't doing a good job of playing into her fantasy. But he wanted her to know how the real world was. It wasn't just some easy thing you could skip through. At least not for them.

"But what would we look like if we were fish? I think I'd wanna be purple and flat and small so I could fit anywhere I wanted. And I'd wanna have wings so I could swim sometimes and fly outta the water when I wanted to go someplace else. It'd probably be boring being in the water all the time." Claudia sniffed. She bit into the fingers of her glove.

"Sounds like you've got fish life all figured out. What would I look like?"

"Hmm. You'd be big and silver. And you'd have muscle fins so you could swim fast and save us. And it'd be better than now 'cause with fins you couldn't wear boxing gloves so you couldn't fight. And then they wouldn't take me away."

"We're far away from the bad people who kept taking you away. I did everything I could to get us as far from them as possible. And I'm not boxing anymore. I'm looking for different work, you know that."

"I just don't want you to come home all hurt anymore. It makes me sad to see you with all the bruises. And your cuts are gross and scary sometimes."

It was true. Sometimes he'd get cut real deep, and it would continue to open as the rounds wore on. As his opponent focused on the gaping wound with jab after jab, followed by heavy crosses and hooks. Hoping to get a TKO stoppage because of all the blood.

"But you know I toughed those out. You saw me after. You saw I was all right."

Claudia folded her arms. "I don't like it. It's not fun watching you hurt," she said.

"Look, I'm healed now. You're doing fine, I'm doing fine. Let's not worry about it. We can think instead about me getting that library job. Then we'll have something. Get a place of our own in a good part of town. You'll see. It'll really happen this time."

Claudia didn't look convinced.

"I'm not boxing now, am I?"

She looked down.

"Am I?"

"No."

"Well, so be happy with that."

She didn't say anything.

"Hey," he said.

She looked up.

"How about you tell me more about the fish world. Something else about us as fish."

"I don't wanna anymore."

"Okay. What about some food?" He raised the sack of

supplies.

"Okay," she said.

"Let's keep going for a bit. There's a place I wanna show you, and I figured we could have a little picnic there."

"It's too cold."

"We make our own rules," Trucks said. "No weather ever stopped us, did it?"

Claudia didn't respond.

"How about a smile, Pepper Flake?"

Claudia looked away. Trucks led the way forward along the bending Yellowstone River up into Two Moon Park. He'd seen it on a map of town pasted to the wall of the shelter lobby. Something about the name drew him to it.

It was disappointing inside the park. Trucks hadn't thought about the winter stripping the branches of leaves, flower stems withered into the ground, the snow covering the usually vibrant grass. They walked around a while and cut through paths until they found a bench. Trucks used his coat sleeves to sweep the snow off the benches and tabletop. They sat across from each other. Trucks opened a bottle of water and handed it to her. She drank a third of it. He cut the apples and spread peanut butter on the slices. They each took one and raised them up.

"To getting that job at the library," he said.

"The spaceship," she said.

Afterward, still hungry, Trucks pulled out the bag of crackers and spread peanut butter on them too. They bit into the crackers in silence and warily looked around at the bare trees lining the park. Trucks let Claudia lick the knife clean.

As they walked out of the park, Trucks took her hand. She was reluctant, but he was glad she didn't pull away. The river alongside them was still and hard.

Out of nowhere, Claudia said, "I'm glad we're not fish."

They walked a bit in silence.

"Why do you say that?" Trucks asked.

"If we're people, we can go anywhere. The fish are stuck. And I know I said I wanna be a flying fish, but I've never seen one. Maybe they're real somewhere, but I don't know. I like that you showed me we can go anywhere and do lots of things. But sometimes it makes me sad. And sometimes I have bad dreams. I guess it would be good being a fish 'cause I don't think they dream. I don't know if they could when they have to swim all the time so they don't die, and probably they don't sleep. And I wouldn't like it if all I did was swim and run away from bears and fishermans and snakes, like you said. It wouldn't be fun. And maybe 'cause you'd be a bigger fish with muscles the fishermans would see you better and wanna catch you. And I'd be alone, and it'd be dark, and I'd be at the bottom of the river hiding."

Trucks squeezed her hand as they walked. He didn't know what to say. So he said, "I meant to bring you out here to show you something pretty. The river and the big park. I just had a lot on my mind. I didn't think about it being winter and everything being dead and buried and frozen and all."

They walked in silence. He kept hoping the sun would come out of the clouds, just a small piece of it, but it didn't. All along the road back, he couldn't stop staring at the bare trees lining the way. Their dark branches like withered arms praying to the sky.

THE DEEP SICK PARTS

In bed that night he dreamed. When he woke in the dark, it was nothing he could remember. Like he was dreaming in shapes without words. The twisting origami inside his mind. Nothing he could put together.

Trucks sat up in his cot. He put his face in his hands and rubbed his eyes. Then he looked over at Claudia. This time she was sleeping faced away from him. She didn't start out that way. He figured she'd turned in the night during a bad dream. The scratchy blanket was half off her. He reached over and pulled it back until she was covered again. He hated how harsh and itchy the material was and wished he could give her something more. Something better.

He watched her sleep, knowing that to be grateful was key. To appreciate the little they had now. To be thankful for all those who'd reached out and helped them so far.

Trucks bent down and sifted through Claudia's coat until he found the copper coin. He couldn't make out the meadowlark or the cutthroat in the dark. Instead he ran his fingers over the embossed metal. Felt the flying of the bird. The swimming of the fish. What it was to be free. He breathed in deep and put the coin back.

The nighttime hum filled the room. There was a louder chorus of snoring than he'd heard before. It was strange sleeping again in a mass of broken humanity. He wondered if anyone else was awake. He tried to look around, but it was dark. The nightlights had been taken again. He wondered if they were ever returned. It was one of those stupid things he thought of in the dark when there was nothing to do but contemplate as he lay beside his girl. Trucks always tried hard not to think of boxing and Elle and June and Gerald and all the pieces of the hard life he'd cobbled together. Not something to brag about. Maybe something to be ashamed of. He really didn't know.

He rose out of bed. He hadn't moved around the room in the night before. Dozens of bunks lining either side of the walls. A walkway down the middle. A door at one end and a row of covered windows at the other.

Trucks walked down the middle aisle. He touched each metal bunk frame as he passed. Nobody stirred. Nothing seemed to move. But he could imagine the rising chests. The way he'd seen his own go in and out against the old mirror back in the boxing gym. And he could see the heaving chests of all those men he'd laid flat, eyes rolled back, mouthpieces hanging off a lip. It depended on how bad he'd slugged them. Hinged on the force of the punishment. The power in the movement. *Pah-pah-pah.* What had he caught them with? Everything. Every damn punch in his arsenal. And they'd gone out stiff. Arms thrust above heads or tucked at the waist. Stiff like mummies. But shaking. Always that quaking in the limbs. The body in the shock of its existence. So much force meeting all that bone and brain. Rattle, rattle. The hard impact of a pugilist life.

When he got to the end of the aisle, Trucks pulled aside

one of the thick curtains. Pulled it just enough so he could
see out. Have a crack at the world. He blew his breath on
the glass and looked at the fog. He wiped the fog away and
blew again. It was a strange sensation fogging up the world
like that. If it weren't for the streetlights, he'd see nothing out
there. He was aware of this. But even under the lamp glow,
he saw nothing. It was a cold, gray world under so much ice
and snow.

Trucks pressed a hand against the glass. The pane was
frosted over. His skin felt nearly numb. The shock of it put a
spark in his belly. And he thought about all those poor boys
lying on the cold canvas. Their backs against that powder
blue, arms spread, eyes closed. Like they were flying through
some absurd fist-socking sky.

He thought about that rush he always felt after he'd
clipped an opponent with his dynamite. Something he'd
never talked about, but they all knew what it was. Had felt
it at some point or another. The ultimate connection of
knuckle to jaw or cheek or temple. The shock of the contact.
The swift movement forward to pounce with combinations.
Those blood-smelling instincts like they were all sharks in
leg-walking human skin. He didn't talk about the high in the
head and the heart whenever the ref pointed him to a neutral
corner. Turned and started the count. Like that faux-flying
boy on the canvas was ever going to stand.

It was real late now. Trucks didn't know the time. But
if his body ever woke him from a nightmare, it was always
three in the morning. No other time. The naturopath had
told him years ago that he woke because of his liver fire. Like
a sickness down so deep he needed to use the strength of all

his energies to work it out. And he'd taken shot after shot to his body in exactly that place, but she'd said that wasn't it. That the body shots weren't the problem at all. That he needed to look far into himself. Scan his emotions. Find all those sick places he didn't understand or was too afraid to look at.

Trucks took his hand off the window. The curtain fell back into place, covering the outside light. His palm tingled in the warmth of the room. The frigid glass so harsh that his hand felt almost hot now. Like his fist was burning up.

Trucks stepped to walk away, then turned back and pulled the curtain aside once more. He just wanted another look and imagined he could see the wind blowing under the low streetlights. But he knew that wasn't true. You couldn't see the wind. But still. Somehow over the humming in the room he could hear the wisps out there. Like the world was saying it was coming for him. It was inching closer. And the deep, sick parts of him told the world to bring it and load up with all its best shots. And he felt a warm sensation down in his abdomen after that. Like all he ever was was ready for it. And all the rest of that night he kept walking away from the window and coming back. Telling himself it was just for one more look. Only one. And then he'd make it to a place of peace. That at some point, he really would.

GERMS OF THE DARK AND LIGHT

After breakfast they sat in the shelter lobby again. Trucks had his hands folded between his knees. He stared down into the space between them like he was in a trance. Claudia picked at the edges of her chair. She'd put on the perfume too thick again and smelled so much like June that it gave him a headache.

Whenever the phone rang, Trucks looked up. But no calls had come for him since he'd filled out his application at the library. Still. There was a warmth in him when he thought about the job. The promise of hope.

Trucks turned to Claudia.

"How's the breakfast settling?" he asked.

"Good. I liked the cereal and juice."

"Me too," he said. But he hadn't eaten any of it. He'd drunk a water and taken some fruit and oatmeal, but all he'd done was stir it around. He still had the night on his mind. Sometimes he just missed the old days too much. When everything was simpler. Or maybe just in retrospect it seemed that way. When his days were about popping the bags and his nights about having a drink or two with the boys. Even a few smokes if he thought his wind was good enough from all the running. Roadwork is what the boys called it. And he did miss the road work. The *tah-tah-tah-tah-tah-tah-tah-tah* of his foot slaps against the pavement. Pushing the body to breathe against the cold, the heat, any damn condition nature could throw his way.

Claudia smelled her hands.

"We didn't wash," she said.

"What?"

"After the breakfast." She pointed at his pocket.

Trucks had forgotten to take out the antibacterial wipes. It wasn't like him. He reached into his coat pocket and pulled out the sachet. It was much lighter now, nearly empty. He handed her a wipe but didn't take one for himself. He watched to make sure she scrubbed hard. Then he borrowed the wipe and cleaned his hands and wrists until there was no moisture left. Trucks stood and walked over to the trash can. He threw the wipe away and came back.

"At least we had our hot showers before we ate," he said. "That should have killed all the germs."

"Are germs ever good?" Claudia asked. "Why do we always kill them?"

"I don't know. I'm not a scientist."

Claudia laughed.

"That funny?"

"Yeah. You don't look like one."

"No, I sure don't," he said.

Trucks found it hard to imagine himself in any skin but what he was. A boxer with a lean body and a cracked nose. A bend in the bridge like all the other boys. But he'd taken care of Claudia with those breaks. Earned enough money with his churning fists and shuffling feet. At least it was a trade. At least it was something. But he couldn't think like that anymore. He needed to remember the warm feeling about the library. The possibility of a newfound life. Something golden he could give to his girl without the pain and the bruising and all those worried looks.

"But the germs," he finally said. "I imagine there are good ones. Something has to fight the bad ones, and I think in nature there's a balance. And to keep that balance, something has to fight them. It can't just be that people came along and invented antibacterials, and that was it. Germs existed since, I don't know, millions of years."

"Millions?"

"Sure. How old do you think things are?"

"I don't know," she said. She looked at her hands. She counted to herself. "A thousand years?"

"People have been keeping dates far longer than that, Pepper Flake."

"Oh."

Trucks patted her leg.

"What do you think? Are there good germs out there fighting the bad ones?" he asked.

"Hmm. But what if they don't fight? What if they work together, like friends? And the bad germs and good germs belong all over the world, and everything only works 'cause they get along. And sometimes when they fight, then people get sick. Cause when they're fighting, nothing feels good."

"I never thought about it like that," he said.

"Yeah," she said.

"You're a clever girl," he said.

"I am?"

"Yeah. And you'll do good things when you grow up. I'll

hope a lot for you, but I won't pressure you to do anything. It's your life, and I'll want you to live it how you want. Probably why I haven't taught you boxing or anything. As much as I'd love to see you throw a hook, it's maybe not in your best interest."

"What do you mean?" she asked. "I could do it, I bet."

"Of course you could. I just mean. Well, you're a lot more delicate. You're tough, that's for sure. There's not a question about that. And you could do it well. Hell, I'm sure you could do anything well. I just wouldn't wanna see you hurt, is all."

"But you do it, and you get hurt a lot."

"That's true."

"So I could do it."

"Of course," he said. Then he thought for a moment. "But remember how you didn't wanna chop that piece of wood back at Gerald's?"

"Yeah."

"Well, I don't know. Sorta like that, I just can't imagine you doing anything that would hurt something. Even if it's for sport. Even if there's a god-awful bunch of beauty to it."

"I wouldn't wanna hurt anything. Not unless I was real mad. 'Cause sometimes when I'm mad I get a hot feeling and wanna hit stuff."

"Boy, do I know that feeling."

She looked at him like she was trying to read his face. "And it's bad?" she said.

Trucks thought it over.

"Just something a person has to learn to control, that's all. I'd ask you what you wanna be when you grow up, but I think that's a stupid question."

"How come?"

From the counter, the woman said, "Mr. Kadoka. Excuse me, over here."

Trucks didn't respond at first. He wasn't used to hearing his false name.

"Mr. Kadoka, the library's on the phone for you."

Trucks snapped out of it and stood.

"Stay here, Pepper Flake," he told Claudia, excitement in his voice.

Then he walked up to the desk and took the phone. He nodded a few times. Switched the receiver from one hand to the other. It didn't take long, and he handed the receiver back to the woman to hang up the phone. Trucks breathed in deep. He rubbed his fist against his leg as he stared out the window. The white of the snow so lit, it was almost blinding.

Trucks walked over to Claudia and held out his hand. She took it without saying anything. He walked her over to the opportunities board. He tried to say something, but nothing came out. Everything around him went muffled. A blur. He started to shake and let go of her hand. The fire in his belly rose. And the next thing he knew he was ripping the opportunities board off the wall and smashing it with his dark boots.

THE DEVASTATION WORDS

Staff members at the home had tried to subdue him, but Trucks blasted the two males with vicious punches. He'd hit one with a crushing liver shot that sent the guy to his knees. The other he'd knocked out with a short hook to the jaw. The guy's arms flew up over his head and stuck there even after he hit the ground. Like the stiff branches of a human tree. And Trucks knew he'd gone overboard when he shoved the woman who came from behind the counter. And with the woman retreating behind the counter, trembling as she called the cops, the two male workers laid out on the floor, Trucks did the only thing the civilized world had taught him to do: run.

They walked at a fast pace. Trucks held Claudia's hand tight. They had left the navy duffel bag and the secondhand clothes and food and water behind. Claudia was in tears. He couldn't worry about it now. They were zipping through the early morning streets of Billings toward Swift Thrift. Trucks didn't have time to think. He shook out his free hand as they walked. Felt the burn along his knuckles. He didn't need to look at them to know they'd turned red with swelling. He could feel it in the pulsing of his hands and that burn in his gut. He wished he could say he felt sorry or remorseful or some other bullshit thing the court would make him say.

But it wouldn't be true. He felt damn good. He was alive again.

Claudia tried to talk as they hurried down the street. Trucks considered his longer legs would do twice her strides and tried to keep beat with her small movements. But she was distraught and confused and trying to talk it out.

"Not now," he'd said when she first said something. Right after they'd shot out of the rescue mission like flickering comets. He didn't comprehend anything she'd said after that. His sole focus on getting away and trying to calm his body after the adrenaline dump. But it was hard to breathe in the cold while moving so fast.

"Why'd you do that?" Claudia asked.

"Hush," he said. "This isn't the time for talk. We're getting some supplies and getting the fuck outta this place."

"But why? Why?! I don't wanna go!"

"I said it's not the time for talk. Shut up a minute and keep moving. The only thing you need to be thinking right now is *go, go, go, go, really fucking go*."

Her sobs grew louder. Trucks pushed the pace. He was sure the police were out looking for them by now. But it was just an assault. It couldn't be anything to get that worked up about. Far worse had to happen in Billings. Or maybe not. What did he really know of civilized places?

When they reached Swift Thrift, Trucks pulled Claudia into an alley beside a dumpster. They were nearly hidden from the main street. He leaned her up against the bricks. Then he got down on a knee at her level and tried to look her in the eyes. Claudia wiped her tears and sobbed. Trucks gripped her shoulders. He squeezed them and rubbed up

and down to comfort her and give her warmth. She kept
trying to hide her face. Looking at all angles. Any direction
that would keep her out of eye contact.

"You gotta look at me, Pepper Flake," he said.

She stared at the ground. It really pissed him off.

"Look, this is one of those now-or-never times. You wanna know about the good and the bad and who deserves the
punishment and who gets off fine and what the fuck this
world is made of? We talk about all that stuff a lot, don't we?
Well, let me burst that bubble completely—it's shit, Pepper
Flake. It's a big spinning globe of shit out there. Few people
care enough about people like us to even looks us in the eyes.
June and Gerald are good people. Really good people, yeah.
But don't believe for a second that when the time came they
wouldn't throw us back out on the street with a 'good luck'
and an 'I did what I could.' A few minutes of warmth and
pats on the back and good karma for them. You think it's
about us? You think it's ever about our well-being? Look at
me."

He took her by the chin. She closed her eyes tight. She
grabbed his wrist with both hands and tried to pull away.

"Look at me. This is important. This is for you. This is
for your future."

She struggled against him. After a while, Trucks just
wrapped her in his arms. She tried to squirm out of his grip,
but he held her tighter. Kept her from going. Claudia cried
on. The more she cried and squirmed, the tighter he held
her. He was utterly losing her in those moments. The vibration of her wails against his body. All the pain and loss she'd
already suffered streaming out of her. The little energy she

had left. And he held her that way for a long time. A light snow falling around them. The city subdued by shifting gray clouds.

And then it was silent. A startling thing.

Trucks pulled away and looked at Claudia. He kept his hands on her shoulders just in case. But she didn't seem ready to run. Her eyes were dark red from all the crying. The lashes askew. Her face pink from the cold and the bitter taste of the world.

Trucks let go. He stared at his girl.

Claudia breathed in stutters. After a while she got her breath back. Everything since the children's home had beaten her down.

In a soft voice, she said, "I wanna go home."

Trucks said, "I know it's probably not what you wanna hear, especially now, but this is it. *This. Me.* I'm all the home you got."

Claudia was drained of life and glow and feeling.

"Wisconsin was just somewhere we were. Born there or not. Raised there or not. It was familiar out of habit. We've been around, me and you. Do you really think there's any place for us? That we could pull out a map and close our eyes and point and find someplace that wants us? Where we finally fit? Where they accept us for what we are or what we've done or what we wanna do? Do you think that's really out there? Because if you do, then all right. If you do, then I'll make that happen. Just tell me. You tell me what you want, and we'll do it."

Claudia shook her head. She leaned back against the wall. She sniffled a few times and rubbed her nose.

"I don't think I want you to be home anymore," she said.

Trucks put his hand to his mouth. His whole body shook. It was the kind of pain that can't be expressed in word or image.

"I...I know I really fucked up this time," he said.

"You lost all our stuff! Gerald's coin and the perfume. I'll never smell her again! And you hurt people. And you were bad to that woman. And you looked like mean guys in the movies."

Trucks turned to the side and threw up. Claudia jumped away. He coughed and wiped his mouth on his sleeve. Then he looked at her again.

"I've really messed this up," he said. "I've done it all wrong. I've been nothing but a failure, when all I've tried to do is what I thought was good and right for you."

She didn't say anything. She kept her distance.

"God, this pain. It hurts so much," he said. "Is there anything I can do, Pepper Flake? There has to be something. I'll find us a good place in an all-right town. Even if nobody wants us, we'll be together. I haven't left. I promised I wouldn't go, and I'm still here. I'm here. Look, see? I'm here. It's so important for you to see that and know that and realize...just realize all I've done to try to build a good kinda life for you." He started to cry. Like it was just hitting him now. "And I just...I can't have you feeling this way about me, Pepper Flake. I can't. I just can't."

Trucks shook uncontrollably. He turned and fell back against the bricks. Sat there in the snow with his girl a few feet away. Staring at him. Watching him fall apart.

"I'm gutted, Pepper Flake. Just so gutted. You know what

that means? You know what it means for a person to be gutted?"

She shook her head.

"It means all they've lived for has been ripped out of them. That life essence. That thing we carry that glows so strong when we're young. And...and starts to fade as we grow. Blinks here and there like it's gonna flicker out. I'm so damn sick. I've done it all wrong, and I don't even know what to do anymore."

Trucks shook and cried hard. He put his hands over his face because he never wanted her to see him break like this. He wished she didn't have to.

Time blurred as he cried into his hands. Not understanding the noises he was making. Feeling like the beast he'd never wanted to become. His shaky hands covering his face. His eyes closed. Images of his life passing quickly like flipped pages. *Twap-twap-twap-twap-twap.* Mother—gone. Father—gone. Elle—gone. First punch. *Pah.* All those blows landed. *Pah-pah-pah-pah-pah*—devastation. All those blows taken. *Pah-pah-pah-pah-pah*—remuneration. The black eyes and the blood and the cracked bones. The movement. The breath. And then his girl. Claudia—redemption.

He didn't know if minutes had passed. Time had sped and slowed. He wiped his eyes and looked over to where Claudia had been. But there was no trace of her. She was gone.

Trucks barely had the heart to react. But he breathed in hard with all that was left. His chest hurt. When he moved to stand and go after her, he heard a sound beside him. Trucks turned, and there she was.

Claudia sat down with her back to the dumpster.

Trucks was overwhelmed with relief. He sat in the snow and just looked at his girl for a while. And his girl looked back at him. They looked in each other's eyes like they were afraid to use words.

Finally, Trucks said, "I'm nothing if not your home. And I might be a fuck-up and do things wrong a lot, but know I've always tried hard for you. None of this has been easy. And I know all this going is a weight on you. But it's all I know. And I still think…well, maybe it's just foolish, but I still think I can make us something good. And if not us, if you don't want me around anymore, then at least find you something good in the hands of someone who can do better. But really, I'll try whatever you wanna try. And maybe I'm just crazy, but I feel like all roads are open until we've got no more breath in us. And if we can just get out there again and try, who knows? Maybe my heart could change about this shit-pile world."

Trucks looked down at the veins running over his hands. The ligaments disappearing whenever he clenched his fists. It was his fuck-ups he could never get over. The way he pulled others down when he never meant to. All those blocks in his mind from his aching heart and the loss of people he'd loved or never got the chance to.

"Mama," she said.

Trucks looked up.

"What?" he said.

"Tell me about Mama."

"Talking about her won't do you any good, Pepper Flake. It'll only bring sadness to your heart."

"Cause it'll hurt?"

"Yes."

"Cause she did bad to us?"

"Because she chose other things."

"Like what?"

"It's not something to talk about now."

Claudia scratched the snow with a finger. Then she looked up, took the oversized gloves off, pulled out both of her hearing aids, and handed them to Trucks. She blew warm air into her hands, then put her gloves back on. "Tell me now," she said. "Tell me so I know but it won't hurt."

"But you won't hear any of it," he said.

Claudia pointed to her ears. She couldn't hear him.

"Just say it," she said. "Tell me the other things. Tell me about Mama."

Trucks held out his shaking left hand. The one he'd busted three times. Now swollen from the punches. Claudia folded her arms. She refused to reach out.

Trucks pulled his hand back. Sat up straight. Cleared his throat.

"Your mama was a hooker and an addict. I hate to say that's all she was, but it's what she became. What she made herself into. At least all I knew of her. Why I fell for her and all that is another story. It's not for now. But there's some good I can say about her. Like she went through with having you, even though she'd never wanted kids. But it was clear there was gonna be something special about you. So she pushed on, and she had you. And you two got the same hair. All those long, dark curls. It's incredible. You wouldn't think two people could look so much alike. And I was always struck by her green eyes. Like shining emeralds. Like she was some starlet or something out of those old movies. And she had an energy about her. Infectious. The kind of thing you felt you'd die about if you weren't around to feel it. And that's probably why I kept by her so long. But the hard stuff is that she never drew to you. She didn't even barely try to be a mother. I'd tell her she had to try, that so much was in the trying, but she'd just go out and get all messed up. She'd promised to quit turning tricks and took this job waiting tables at a diner, but it wasn't long before she went back to working the streets. She probably never really quit in the first place. But I wanted to believe she had. But she really probably didn't. And most nights it was just me and you alone in that old rowhouse by the train tracks. Me feeding you all them mushed bananas and peas and carrots. And that old train. You probably don't remember the train going through. Passing all those times. How I'd hold you to my chest so you could feel my heart going. Close my eyes and dance you around the room so you wouldn't cry because of all the shaking walls. And I'd hold you, and we'd dance, and I'd pretend it was me and you out on that big old train. Rolling wherever the tracks took us. So many miles from all the bad we knew. Riding all the curves and bends and passing the open fields of the world. All that opportunity. All that hope. And your mama. She started being gone for longer. The stretches of time widening. Days to weeks. Weeks to months. And soon she was utterly gone. Like all I'd ever loved was a memory. And now it's hard to remember anything but the bad things. Her drunk breath. Crushing up pills in the kitchen with a soup can so she could snort it off the counter. And

how many johns she had in that time, I wouldn't even count.
I don't even wanna think of it. She left us, Pepper Flake. She
just took off and left us for the booze and drugs and street
cash, and that's really all I'm trying to say. And maybe she
was never nothing better than a strung-out hooker. I don't
know. It's what the boys from the gym would say sometimes
when they'd had enough to drink to get loose. And I knew it
was true, I guess. But I still told them all to shove it or make
a move. Because nobody was gonna talk about my family
that way. But she never really was family. It makes the word
feel abused when using the word like that. But she carried
you and gave you life. And for that I'm so thankful. And
what you are inside is nothing like me and nothing like her.
You came from somewhere else. Like the world knew you'd
be fucked to all hell if you were too much like either of us.
So it gave us you. No. It gave *me* you. And whether or not
I can see hints of your mama or me in your personality, it
doesn't really matter. It doesn't matter at all. Because you're
you. And it's been the joy of my life to get to know you. And
I'll tell you that sometime. If you'll have me. If you'll keep
me around. And maybe I'm nothing but poison to you, even
if all I wanted was to be your home. And maybe I just need
to find someone who can do better for you. It's clear I don't
know a damn thing about how to do this. But I've tried, and
I always hope you get that. But anyway. So that's the story
of your mama. A regular southside Klakanouse hooker who
chose addiction over me and you and left us. It eats me up
to even think of it. And she's probably dead by now, but I'd
never tell you that. But anyway, that's the truth about her.
That's all there really is."

Trucks went quiet.

Claudia nodded.

Trucks leaned forward to hook the hearing aids over her ears. Claudia pulled away. Then she took off her gloves and held out her hands. Trucks put the hearing aids on her palms, and Claudia struggled to put the earmolds in. But after a while, she got them in.

"What'd it sound like?" he asked. "When I was talking and you couldn't hear."

"Like when you're underwater and all you hear is blurry stuff," she said.

"Did you feel anything?" he asked. "About what I said?"

"I just watched your face with the blurry stuff."

Trucks moved like he was going to sit beside her against the cold dumpster. Claudia shook her head.

"You think sometime you can forgive me?" he asked.

Claudia didn't say anything.

They sat there for minutes in silence. Watched their breaths go out. Trucks rubbed his knuckles against his hip. Then he put his hands in his coat pockets. Claudia stared at the brick wall across the alley.

"Tell me a story about why Mama's gone," Claudia finally said. "So I can have something good to remember for now."

Trucks thought a minute. Then he remembered a theory he'd heard about once.

"Your mama's gone because she's on Mars," he said. "It's a planet way far out. They suspected there was water up there, and since there was maybe water the scientists said life could exist. So all the space programs in the world got together and started a mission to send people into outer space and all the

way to Mars. They wanted to colonize the planet because it
hadn't been done before. So they searched the whole world
looking for only a thousand people to go live on Mars. Can
you imagine? A thousand people out of billions. And they
knew they had to find the most unique and special people
because they wanted to make a good impression on the universe. And so the space programs taught them all about the
galaxy and how to space farm and sew space clothes and talk
in a totally new language so they could survive on another
planet. Then after years of hard training they loaded all the
special people on ten huge spaceships and thrust them into
outer space. Hurled your mama past the moon. And that's
where she is right now. Probably smiling down at you from
that red planet, hand on her heart, real proud and happy like
a goddamn space clam."

MODIFIED KARMA

Before they went into Swift Thrift, he explained it to her direct.

"We're gonna need borrow worse than we did before. We don't have enough money to pay for supplies and eat. So we have to make a choice. We either pay for everything and don't eat, or we need borrow from the store and eat. What do you wanna do?"

"That's all we can choose?"

"That's all we can choose."

"Need borrow and eat, I guess."

"It's a good choice."

"It kinda feels like no choice is a good choice."

"Now you're learning," he said.

They turned the corner and walked into the store. Swift Thrift hadn't been open long. A few customers sifted items on the shelves. A couple of old guys clanged gardening tools. A woman browsing candleholders sniffed empty glass jars.

Trucks walked Claudia over to the luggage section. Suitcases, briefcases, laundry bags. The best he could find was a cloth tote bag. He folded it up, looked around, and got down on a knee.

"I need you to come through for us," he said. "Do you understand?"

"How?" she asked.

He knew they wouldn't suspect a little girl of taking things.

"Put this in your coat like you did with the T-shirt the other day. Then follow me around the store. I'm gonna pick things off the shelf and hand them to you. We're gonna do this in secret. When nobody's watching, you'll put these things inside your coat too. And look all around before you put it in there. Make sure nobody's watching you. Maybe think of it like looking both ways before you cross the street. So you don't get hit by something."

"I don't wanna," Claudia said.

"What?"

"I don't wanna do bad anymore."

"This isn't bad. I told you. Don't you remember? We don't wanna do these things. We have no choice. Sometimes we're forced to need borrow. Okay?"

Claudia looked away.

"Listen, remember, when we're living an all-right life somewhere, we'll pay it all back. We'll donate to the local charities and serve food at the soup kitchens. It's like that karma we talked about. Right here, the world's giving to us, and we're accepting. That's positive karma for the world. Then later, we'll give back, so that's returning the karma. Like a thanks for the need borrowing."

Claudia shrugged. "Not in my coat. I don't wanna."

Trucks stood. He shook his head and walked over to the clothing area. Then he unzipped his coat, took a pair of children's thermal tights, and stuffed them inside.

"You need some earmuffs?" he asked.

"I don't know."

"I thought the hearing aids might make your ears colder. The hard plastic and everything," he said.

Claudia reached up and fidgeted with the hearing aids as if she was testing the hard shells.

Trucks grabbed a pair of earmuffs. They were purple and fuzzy. He squeezed the muffs. He worried the hard, plastic wire might press too much on her head and the muffs might push her hearings aids against her ears. Maybe cause more discomfort than warmth. Trucks put the earmuffs back and found a winter headband. Looked like it was handknitted from a strong yarn.

"How about this?" he said.

Trucks handed Claudia the headband. She put it on.

"It's warm," she said.

Trucks took the headband back, looked around, then stuck it in his coat.

"We'll need a sleeping bag. Come on."

Trucks walked to an area with old lanterns, kindling, tents. He went through their assortment of sleeping bags. Not as many as he'd expected being in Montana where Gerald said everyone cherished the outdoors. Trucks chose the thinnest sleeping bag because it'd be easier to carry and sneak out with. It was dark green, and the tag said it held heat at twenty degrees. It would have to do.

"They called them rollie blankets," Claudia said.

"What? Who did?"

"At the home."

"Never heard them called that."

"It was their words."

"You're thinking of the home?"

Claudia looked away.

Trucks rolled up the sleeping bag as tight as he could.

"What are you thinking of the home for?"

"I miss playing with Suzie and Mary and Connie. I miss Mary most. She was nice to me most times."

Trucks found a stuff sack lying on the shelf and put the sleeping bag in there. It really wasn't all that big when compressed like that.

"What'd you say?" Trucks asked.

"I miss Mary most. It was good there sometimes."

"Look, I didn't mean to take you away from your friends, but how else could I make you a better life? Don't you think that's where we're headed?"

Claudia didn't answer.

"Is that where you'd rather be now? At the home?"

Claudia ran her finger along the thin fabric of a sleeping bag.

Trucks didn't even want to think about it.

"Let's get out of here," he said. "We've borrowed enough."

Trucks tucked the compressed sleeping bag in the stuff sack under his arm.

"Promise we can get the camera back," Claudia said.

Trucks looked around.

"Promise," she said again.

"I think the karma gods can forgive this one," he said, and grabbed her hand.

Trucks walked a slow stride past the register counter. When he thought they'd made it safely, almost to the door, Claudia jerked from his grasp and yelled, "Liar!"

The woman at the register looked over. "What's going on?" she said.

Trucks grabbed Claudia's hand and squeezed hard. He shoved the door open and dragged her onto the sidewalk. He looked down at her with fire in his eyes, and said, "Run, goddammit, if you know what's good for you."

MOONLIGHT POLLUTION

The two flickering comets had run through the wall of cold. Sprinted down the street, breathing hard as they ran the stretches and turned the corners. The taste of blood had filled their throats. Tongues metallic. Trucks had led them north to Swords Park, a place he'd spotted on the wall map back at the shelter. It was the closest place he could remember, and the harsh conditions of the park would have to do.

They'd spent most of the day hiding. After running so hard they walked to a small picnic site and hid for hours. There was a bathroom hut nearby and a picnic table under a gazebo. Trucks said they'd make camp there later on. When they got hungry, Trucks led Claudia to a grocery store. They paid for bread and peanut butter and a few bottles of water. He didn't feel right need borrowing all the time, and he'd told her that repeatedly, but she didn't seem to believe him now. They were down to thirteen dollars. When they'd returned to their spot in Swords Park, he'd reached in his coat pocket for the sachet of antibacterial wipes, but they weren't there. He'd lost them in the scuffle back at the shelter. Instead they washed their hands in the bathroom hut. The hot water never came, and just using hand soap from a dispenser on the wall didn't make Trucks feel clean enough. They made peanut butter sandwiches at the picnic table and drank their waters fast and refilled them in the bathroom sink. Then they walked along the nearby trail. Trucks tried to forget about how she'd turned on him at the store. He'd been pissed and wanted to spank her, but the run had taken a lot out of him. He'd been able to calm himself with breathing techniques and later showed Claudia the gray rimrocks overlooking the city. Though she didn't seem interested and kept trying to look at other things. Still. Trucks had tried to make up a story about how the jagged formation was shaped thousands of years ago and paint the image of what the wildlife was like. But he didn't have the heart or mind for it. For the first time since they'd left Klakanouse, he couldn't get up the energy or desire to teach her. To tell her his version of the making of the world.

It got dark fast. Trucks opened the pull string on the stuff sack and took out the sleeping bag. He unrolled it and shook it out. The tag said it was made of goose-down feathers, which Trucks knew were supposed to be warmer than most. He could see from the glow of the moonlight and the city's light pollution. Their eyes soon got used to it.

"I wanna eat some more," Claudia said, watching him shake the sleeping bag.

"Not tonight."

"But I'm hungry still."

"You just ate a few hours back."

"Still I'm hungry," she said.

"We have to ration now. We're down on money, and you don't wanna need borrow any more than we have to, do you?"

Claudia shook her head.

"Do you?" Trucks repeated. He laid the sleeping bag across the picnic table.

"No," she said.

"I know you're not comfortable with it, so I'm trying to figure out another way. I just don't know what yet. You realize sometimes it just comes to that, right? That you gotta take or freeze or starve or die. It's the way the world works."

"I guess," she said. She walked closer to him and ran her hand across the sleek material of the sleeping bag.

"Can't tell if it'd be better here than in the snow," he said. Then he knocked his fist on the table and walked from under the little gazebo out into the snow. He stomped his boot. "Can't tell which surface is harder. And all this snow on the ground."

Claudia walked over and dug her heel into the snow.

"What do you think?" he asked.

She didn't say anything. Just kept looking at the snow.

He thought about how she'd said she didn't want him to be "home" anymore. It had cut him deeper than anything, the thought of her not wanting to be with him. And now all this pushback and attitude. He didn't know how to handle it.

Claudia bent down and patted the snow.

"I think it's maybe softer here," she said.

Trucks got on his knees. He pushed into the snow. He did it with his bare hands.

"You're cold," she said.

"Why do you say that?"

"Your hands are all red. Like flowers."

"It's not so bad. It's one of those things you get used to."

"Why didn't you borrow gloves?"

"It's not something I thought about. I was only thinking of you." Trucks looked up at his girl. "Anyway, how are those tights feeling?"

"Tight," Claudia said. She pulled the band up out of her black jeans and snapped it back.

"And the headband? Looks like it's not too snug."

Claudia pulled her hood down and put her hands over her ears. "It's really hot. Kinda itchy."

Trucks reached over and pulled her hood back on.

Claudia looked down. She scooped snow, held it over her head, and watched it fall. Her breath came out as she looked at the ground. Trucks could see it sharp against the moonlight.

"So what's it gonna be? In the snow or on the picnic table?"

Claudia stood and walked into the gazebo. She pounded on the picnic table a few times. Then she came back and put her knees in the snow.

"It's dryer in there. And it feels warmer. I don't know. But the snow is pretty."

"So maybe up on the picnic table?" Trucks said.

"Yeah. But I don't wanna be cold."

"It'll be okay," Trucks said. "It'll be cold, but it'll be okay. There's two of us, and we can share the heat. And we got the bag. It can keep us warm down to twenty degrees."

"Twenty degrees?"

"Yeah."

"How cold is that?"

"Pretty damn cold."

"How cold is it now?" She breathed out a puff of breath

and watched it float.

"Also pretty damn cold. But not so cold we'll freeze or anything. We'll be okay."

Trucks stood. He reached out. Claudia shook her head. It hurt him every time she rejected his attempts at connection.

Trucks walked to the gazebo. Claudia followed.

"Just keep all your stuff on. You'll get in the bag first, and I can come after. Sit up here," he said.

Claudia stood on the bench and sat on the picnic table. Trucks smoothed out the sleeping bag along the table top. Then he unzipped the sleeping bag and peeled it open. Then he untied her boots.

"I'm gonna take these off. Get in the bag right after, okay?"

"Okay."

Trucks took off her boots, and Claudia scrambled into the sleeping bag. Then he pulled the flap over her. He took the cloth tote bag with their supplies and held it by the handles. Spun the bag until it was cinched up tight. Then he tied the spun handles to an outside strap on the sleeping bag so it'd be as secure as he could make it and keep it close to them. Trucks sat on the picnic table with his boots on the bench. He untied his boots and took them off. Then he quickly tied them to the loop holding Claudia's boots and the tote bag.

Soon he worked his way into the bag and pulled the dual zipper from the inside nearly up to the neck. Since it was a bag for one adult, it didn't fit right. Just then Trucks realized why the tag had called it a "mummy" bag. There was a gap for the face, and the bag surrounded the whole head and rest of the body. It was a tight fit. They tried to move in different positions, but Claudia could breathe the easiest lying against his chest. It reminded Trucks of the first ride they'd hitched together in the bed of the pickup under the cattle tarp. He breathed in deep with the memory. He looked up at the arched gazebo ceiling. All those beautiful angles. The aura of blue moonlight around it. He could feel the beats of her heart against him. And that was more than enough.

INSIDE THE MUMMY BAG

She woke in the night. Trucks hadn't slept. He was paranoid about winter coyotes and weirdos that lurked in the dark. Both were dangerous for different reasons. He hadn't been too worried at the shelter. Something about the four walls and heat and that slight humming. Like the electric world was praying. But out here it felt like a whole different thing. The way he could hear the wind and feel the snow being blown across the sleeping bag and through the gazebo. It all echoed under there. Like they were lying in a wooden chamber with knocked-down walls.

"You're up," he said.

"I had a nightmare. It really wasn't good," she said.

Her face was on his chest. When she talked, her lips buzzed against him.

"You wanna tell me about it?" he asked.

"No," she said.

"All right," he said.

They lay there in silence. The later it got the more the moonlight seemed to shine blue around them. But Trucks couldn't see much through the face hole. His vision was limited to forty-five degrees. He couldn't look left or right. It hindered his ability to see and feel protected. It made him tense.

"I gotta pee," she said.

"Hold it," he said.

"But I really gotta go."

"It's freezing out there. And I think I hear coyotes."

"Oh no," she said.

"Exactly," he said.

Trucks tried to raise up a bit to have a look out one side of the face hole.

"What is it?" she said.

"Just trying to see what's going on out there."

"Do you see stuff?"

"Not shit," he said.

"The swears," she said.

Trucks laid flat again. He could feel the divide of the boards beneath his back. Sometimes when his spine fell in a groove it'd hurt. He had an aching back from all those years of pivoting on his punches. Like the spine was a pole the body wound around to create the most speed and force. The anchor of the legs. Where all that brute power came from.

"Were you ever really gonna get us a place alone?" she asked.

"Yeah," he said.

"Are you just saying that?"

Trucks tried to picture their own place, but nothing came to mind.

"We won't," she said. "Will we?"

"It's possible," he said.

"I don't believe you," she said.

"Look, I can't promise, and I can't predict. Doesn't mean

I'm not gonna try for you. I hope you feel the trying counts."

She didn't say anything. He felt he offered her nothing but disappointment.

"If we were gonna get a place, where would you want it to be?" he asked.

"I don't know," she said. "I don't really know places."

"That's fair," he said.

"I guess Mown Tinna. Cause we're here already."

Montana. He held back.

"Wouldn't you prefer somewhere warm, like Nevada?"

"Is there snow there sometimes?"

"No. Not in Nevada."

"I was afraid they'd make fun of my hearing phones there. It's not nice if they did that."

"I agree. They shouldn't make fun of you. But you don't know they will. We haven't even gone yet."

"I don't wanna."

"Don't worry, because we probably can't get there without hitching again, anyway, and I know you don't wanna do that. So I don't know if it matters what we want anymore."

Trucks sighed. He felt the weight of her lift with his deep breath.

"What would you want if we could have our own place again?" he asked.

"A room."

"A room?"

"Yeah. For me only."

Trucks could feel how far she'd separated from him. He wondered if a place of their own would bring her back. Would anything now? And could they really stay in Montana? They probably needed to get somewhere else where he wasn't wanted for assault. Or kidnapping, for that matter. He still wondered if anyone in Klakanouse would even care. Just a couple more deadbeats flushed out of the ghetto by the tracks. Probably presumed dead. If they even mattered enough to presume about.

"We could work that out. We could get a place of our own sometime. Sure," he said.

Claudia didn't answer.

"But I think we gotta get outta here first. I know you don't wanna hear it, but we should really hit the road again. I could be in trouble here. I probably am."

"I don't wanna hitch," she said.

"I know," he said.

"You did bad," she said.

Trucks opened and closed his left hand. It was down along the side of the sleeping bag. He had his other arm keeping his girl against him so she wouldn't slip away.

"I did bad," he said. "You're right. Just because we're people doesn't make us better than animals. We might have these brains, but that animal heat, when it kicks in, there's no telling what a man might do. It's why you can't really trust anybody. Aside from me. Remember that. You can always trust me. And remember that the world's a hard place. Or maybe don't remember that. I don't know. But anyway, we'll make it. We will. And I think you know that in your heart."

Trucks tried to look down, but he couldn't see Claudia's face. She was too close against him. He took her silence for sleep, and it stayed quiet that way until morning.

THE DOING HAS NO NAME

In the morning he took her for gas station pancakes. They were spongy and cheap. Claudia loaded them with syrup. Trucks resisted eating. Instead he drank cup after cup of water and bought a pack of antibacterial wipes for seventy-nine cents. They were down to ten dollars. When Claudia went to the bathroom, Trucks stole a couple toothbrushes and a tube of toothpaste and hid them inside the cloth tote bag. He was exhausted from little sleep. All through the night he felt like he heard the calls of the winter coyote, but he could never be sure. Gerald had talked about them back on his property. How he had to kill them some years when they went after his livestock. He'd seemed happy not to have to pick up a rifle anymore. Like the shooting was a part of a violent past he didn't want to think about.

"Let's say we couldn't stay here. Where would you wanna go instead? If we had to," Trucks said.

The sun was cresting. Everything had looked so still and calm after they woke and washed up in the bathroom hut near the gazebo. Now they were sitting across from each other at a small table stuck against the gas station window.

"If we can't stay here?" Claudia asked.

"That's right."

"Cause you were bad?"

"We already went over that. The cops could be looking for us. It might be best if we left."

"Then what can I choose?" she asked.

"I don't know," he said.

Trucks stood and grabbed her pancake box. He tossed her used plastic fork and knife in there along with her wadded-up napkins. Then he took the box over to the trash and threw it away. Trucks grabbed a few packets of plastic cutlery, returned, and put them inside the tote bag. The sleeping bag was in there, too, packed tightly into its stuff sack.

"We could try to get to Nevada," he said, sitting down. "Maybe figure something else out in Montana. A guy back at the shelter told me about a town called Missoula some hours west of here. They got a college and some breweries and nice people. Supposed to be like a blue-collar town with hippies. I don't know. Washington's out that way too. Idaho, I think."

They sat in silence.

"Kinda feels like we're not too close and not too far from things, doesn't it?" he said.

"Sure," she said.

"A tough place," he said.

"Why can't we go see June or Gerald?" she asked. She looked up, sad in her eyes.

"We can't hassle Gerald again. And I really don't think June would be too happy to see us after we took off."

Claudia sighed.

"I know. But we needed to go," Trucks said. He felt he was always having to defend his decisions. All that accountability. The price of being a father.

Trucks opened the packet of wipes. Unscented. He handed one to Claudia. At first she refused, but he made her take
it. She huffed and wiped her hands.

"Up the wrists too," he said.

She wiped her wrists and threw the wipe on the table.
Trucks picked it up, rubbed his hands and wrists.

"But maybe sometime we could see her again," Trucks
said. "It's possible. You never know. We could find where she
lives pretty easy. She practically told me the address."

"I really wish," Claudia said. "But I don't believe you."

"Quit saying that. We can live our lives until then and see
what happens. There's nothing wrong in that. We could have
a pretty interesting life, and I can be just as good as them."

Claudia looked out the window.

"I know we've had some real struggles, but maybe we
don't have to look at is as good and bad. They're just experiences. Just the things we've done. Maybe we don't have
to mark everything with judgments. Sometimes we just do,
and the doing has no name."

"Can't we just go back?" she said, and pointed at the window.

"No fucking way. No more Wisconsin," he said. "We're
never going back. I already told you that. We didn't leave to
give in. We didn't do all this just to go back to that nightmare. I'd lose you for sure. I'd lose you forever."

Trucks looked outside. When people stopped for gas,
they stood with their hands in their pockets waiting for the
tank fill. So used to the cold that they didn't jump back in the
car to get warm. Sometimes they'd do little dances to keep

the heat circulating, and it'd remind him of staying light on his feet in the ring. The movement of circling. The leaning and the leverage and the reaching for range. All things he missed. All things he thought about at any point in the day. All things he needed to get off his mind.

"So maybe Nevada or heading west to Missoula or Washington or Idaho. Gerald was from somewhere in Idaho. I can't remember the name of the town. He learned to box from nuns. Can you believe that?"

"What's a nun?"

"The religious women with the long black outfits and the caps. They're supposed to be sweet, holy people. Good people. They walk with their hands together. Haven't you seen them?"

"I think," she said.

"Well, he learned to box from them. He told me about it."

"He didn't seem like a boxer," she said.

"How do you mean?"

"I don't know. His face wasn't so bad as yours. And he was...he seemed good."

"And I'm not? Look, don't count me out just yet. And my cuts are pretty healed. Bruises gone. Nobody would know. Besides, he boxed a long time ago, when he was young, and maybe he was kinda rough like me then. I don't know. How could I possibly know a thing like that?"

Trucks looked down at his hands. He suddenly felt sad about himself. For no reason he reached up and touched his nose.

"It's all crooked," she said.

"I've taken a lot of shots there."

"It hurts a lot?"

"Usually a while after the break. I've broken it a few times. You got so much adrenaline going during a fight it kills the pain a bit. But maybe for some people it hurts right away. I don't know how the body works for everyone else."

Trucks leaned back. He realized he hadn't closed the bag of antibacterial wipes and sealed the clasp. Then he put the sachet in his coat pocket and folded his hands on the table.

"I don't think anyone's good with pain. Some people can handle it better than others, but I can't imagine anyone wants to be in pain. I do know that some look for it because they think they deserve to hurt, and that's a whole different animal. The mind of man and how it plays tricks on itself. It's a messed-up thing."

Claudia looked confused.

"I don't enjoy the pain, is all I'm saying. And you never fully get used to it. Besides, there's far worse pain than the physical, and I think you're figuring that out. Like it or not. I hope it serves you later in life, Pepper Flake. I really do."

Claudia used her index finger to draw imaginary shapes on the table.

"What's Nevada like?" she asked.

"Never been there. But really warm. A lot of desert. I've seen pictures."

"Do they swim 'cause it's so hot?"

"Sure. Thousands of pools. Probably everyone has a pool because it's so damn hot. And all the buildings have them on the roofs, too, and anybody can use them for free. And they do pool parties all the time with floaty animals and cakes and bubbles and stuff like that."

"I'd like that," she said. After a pause, she said, "But is it real? What you said? You say a lot of things that probably aren't real."

"I don't know if it's real," he said. "The pools and the parties. The rest is true. But they don't have seasons, really, because it's all desert. So you have to think about that. And then it's just hot all the time and really dry. Probably hard for us to breathe there."

"I wouldn't like that. And Mown Tinna's pretty," she said. "Do they have seasons here?"

"Yeah."

"And Washington?"

"I think. I guess I don't really know."

Claudia went back to drawing on the table. Trucks glanced outside. Still had plenty of morning.

"Which way's Mizz Una?"

"West. Everything's west."

"But I really don't wanna hitch again."

"I know. It wears me out, too, Pepper Flake."

"I wanna stay."

"I know. And don't go thinking I like the wandering. I really don't. I think we're just the kinda people who're made for it, and sometimes you just do something for that reason, not because you love it. And anyway, I'm just looking out for you. I'm trying to find you the best life I can."

Claudia stared at the table.

Trucks felt desperate. He said, "I guess maybe if we laid low a while or something."

Claudia looked up.

"Like if we kept quiet and stayed up in that area near the park, maybe it'd be okay for a while. We'd have to eat real cheap and keep rationing, but I guess we could try."

"I wanna," she said.

"It's risky," he said.

Claudia shrugged.

"I don't like it as much as the other options," he said.

"It's what I want," she said.

"This could end badly. Just know that."

THE HOWLING MIND

That night they lay in the sleeping bag on the picnic table. It was a harsh cold. The wind whipped and howled. It blew rough against the bag. Trucks spent the first part of the night humming very low, the sound and vibration calming Claudia. When he felt her jerk in the night, he'd hum again, and she'd relax. Just small sounds. Noises he'd never heard himself make.

Trucks didn't know what time it was. He looked up through the face hole of the mummy bag. Stared at the dark boards in the gazebo's arch. He did everything he could not to wake her. Not to move. But a part of him wanted her to wake because he loved talking with her more than anything. Especially in the night. Those rare moments when maybe they could be more candid. When she sought his protection from the cold and the dark.

Trucks heard a howl. Were the winter coyotes out? Was it just the wind? He imagined they were coming for him. Climbing the rugged hills. Running toward the pathetic campsite. How many could he fend off? A few? Even one? No, probably none. Probably none.

There it was again. Was it howling? Or just the strong-blowing wind?

He'd lain awake over so many long nights. Always Claudia at his side or close by. He remembered lying on the mattress in their one-room rowhouse, staring up at the ceiling. The streetlights casting a sliver of hard orange on the ceiling. He'd watch it until daybreak, gazing at the angled thing like it was going to tell him something. Offer advice or sympathy or friendship. But it just stayed like that. Saying nothing. Offering nothing. Going black when he blinked and always appearing again when he opened his eyes. Claudia an infant, sleeping beside him on the tough mattress. Elle probably only blocks away, whispering in someone's ear. Trucks feeling the ghost of their love so far away that she could have been on another continent. It wouldn't have really mattered.

He ran his hand along the inside of the sleeping bag to his mouth. He kissed his thumb. Then he ran that thumb over Claudia's eyebrow. She didn't stir or wake, breathing in a peaceful way. Face against him. Steady breaths. He wondered if she'd ever truly know how much he cherished her. If his actions and words had revealed that. If in the future they would too. It was the kind of thing that ate at him in the night.

Again he heard the howling. Was it all in his mind? He didn't know. Trucks was exhausted. He was ready to start their new life. But they hadn't been on solid ground for a while. He'd really messed up back at the shelter. He hadn't envisioned himself snapping like that. So he didn't get the job. So he didn't pass their test. All right. Fine. He wasn't smart in their way. But he knew he was clever in the ring. That he was smart about working body to head and back. How to make his opponent expect one style and get another, one combination and get another, one kind of beast and come to a rude awakening with another. Use the speed to counter the fast-flurry punchers, the muscle to counter the speed, the wind to counter the power, the guts and heart to counter the shills.

Trucks shook his head. The boxing like a sickness he couldn't heal. But he loved it so much. Like he loved Elle. Similar kinds of sicknesses, maybe. He didn't know. And did it make him bad? Did it make him wrong? Was there even such a thing as balancing loves like they were good and bad? Just words people had invented to pick sides.

The howling.

Trucks held Claudia tighter. If there was right and wrong, he knew his heart was right about how he loved her. It was the burning ember of anger inside him that he needed to cool. Poked and poked all his life. He'd have to change, or else. He knew that. But now wasn't the time. They were nearly out of money, and he could feel the desperation in his hollow throat. He knew what he had to do, and he'd tell her in the morning. The choice didn't worry him. It was the *or else* that made him shiver. Like a void he couldn't even begin to think about.

ALL THE LIGHT IN THE WORLD

In the early morning Trucks had Claudia wash up in the bathroom hut. Cold water and hand soap to clean her face. Lightly dampened paper towels to clean her body. Trucks did the same when she was done. It was the best they could do. Baring their skins, even inside the cement walls, took a lot of mental strength. It was damn cold.

They brushed their teeth with the stolen toothbrushes. Trucks had nabbed one with soft bristles for her. He didn't mind the hard stuff. As a kid he'd used toothbrushes with bristles made from stiff boar's hair. They'd been donated to the home by a hippie commune. He figured if he and Claudia settled someday, he'd get her a boar's hair toothbrush just for kicks. Tell her more about what it was like growing up near the old smokestacks.

But now they were sitting across from each other at the picnic table. Trucks rubbed his eyes. His throat felt tight.

"Listen. I was thinking all morning of these things I could tell you and how I could put it. Talk about how there's no work and I got no chance around here and the normal life isn't for us and all that. But I'm gonna spare you and give it to you clean. If we're gonna survive and get through this, work toward the kinda life you want with our own place and your own room, then I'm gonna have to get back to boxing."

"What?" She looked afraid.

"It's what I'm good at and what I know. It's where I can make the bills when we need it. After that, I can move on to something else. I can figure out other things."

"No!"

"I don't know what else to do, Pepper Flake."

"No! No! No!"

Trucks reached out, but she pulled away.

"You said you wouldn't anymore. Not again. Not ever again!"

"You don't want me to lie to you, so I'm not lying. I'm telling you straight. If we wanna survive, I need to make money. How else do you think we get food? We can't just keep taking. We're in enough trouble as it is."

"It's your fault! We're in trouble 'cause of what you always do."

"I'm trying my best. I've given what I can. We have to eat. We have to live and survive."

"But you're just gonna get your bruiseity brains hurt. And I'll be alone, and you'll be dead with your brains out."

"I'll fight safer. Smarter. And you won't be alone. I'll always be here."

"Why can't we live with Gerald or June? They were nice and good, and it was better with them. I wanna see them. I don't want you to box. You promised you'd stop. You promised!"

Trucks reached across the table. Claudia scooted away.

"Just until we have enough to get a place and live for real," he said. "It won't be long. A month or two. Just a handful of fights until I make enough to get us a place. You want your own room, don't you? I bet I can get it for you. Rents aren't high here. That's what Gerald said, and you trust him. You liked him. He wanted us to stay here and make a life. So, all right, I'm making us a life. It's just taking some time. It's not easy. This whole damn thing."

Claudia bit into the fingers of her glove and looked away.

The gray morning wouldn't lift. Like all the light in the world had been sucked out.

THE RETURN OF THE WINTER COYOTE

Claudia woke hungry in the night. Trucks got out of the sleeping bag in the bitter cold and left her zipped inside. He rubbed his hands with an antibacterial wipe. Then he made a peanut butter sandwich for her and filled a plastic bottle in the bathroom sink. He came back and rubbed her hands down with a new wipe. She ate the sandwich in the sleeping bag, lying on him. He could feel her chewing against his ribs. When she was thirsty, he fed the water to her. It went like that for a while.

Then she fell asleep. Trucks kept her hooked in his arm. He looked out from the face hole of the mummy bag. The wooden arches of the gazebo always creaking overhead. The wind playing the boards like an old instrument. He thought of the wooden planks under the boxing ring's canvas. His shuffling feet. The blood drips dotting the soft blue like red constellations. *Pat. Pat. Pat.* He could hear the dripping blood of his boxing past. *Pat.*

He didn't want to hurt her. He didn't want to put her through it again. But what else could he do? His mind searched for other possibilities, but there seemed to be none. He could get back in the fight game easy. One stop at the casino. He could get a fight in no time. He could pick up the cash in a day. In a night. Two fists' worth of work.

Trucks closed his eyes. He tried to listen over the wind. There was always something out there. Something roaming. Coming closer.

He pulled his girl in tight and waited for the howl of the winter coyote.

BELLE MARE CASINO

"What do you have there?" the events coordinator asked. He pointed to the cloth tote bag. Trucks was carrying it by the handles. They were standing in the casino lobby.

"The mattress. The fridge. All our possessions. Those kinds of things," Trucks said.

The events coordinator laughed. His shiny gold nametag said *Wendell*.

"I'm here about the fights you put on. I heard you run a couple cards a week. That true?"

"Our venue hosts some boxing extravaganzas each month and a few smaller cards each week. Sometimes it's hard to get the lineups together, but we manage."

"Who arranges the cards, you or the local clubs?"

"A mix of both. Are you a trainer?"

"No."

"Are you looking to sponsor a fighter?"

"You're looking at the fighter."

Wendell smoothed the lapels of his tan suit jacket.

"You're getting up there in age. Maybe a little worse for wear."

"Nose give me away?" Trucks said.

"The scars. Some divots. Hard times?"

"Hard times."

"How old?"

"Thirty-five."

"Let's not bullshit each other here."

"Forty-one."

"Thought about there."

"Good guess."

"Let's see your hands."

Trucks put the tote bag on the carpet and raised his hands.

"Have they taken much damage?" Wendell asked.

"Broke the left three times. No real damage to the right."

"Do you take dives?" Wendell asked.

Trucks dropped his hands and looked over at his girl. Claudia was sitting on a plush chair across the room. He'd told her to stay there because he didn't want her listening to the conversation.

"Never taken a dive," Trucks said. "Is that how these cards go?"

Wendell shrugged. "Sometimes. Most of the fights are legitimate. I just wanted to see what kind of guy we might be working with."

"I'm a guy who takes straight fights. Cash. You got any light-heavy openings?"

Wendell looked Trucks up and down. He pointed at him. "You look more like a middleweight, unless you're going to magically add ten pounds over the next few days."

Trucks hadn't weighed himself in weeks. They weren't eating much. His coat fit looser. His body didn't feel right. What did feel right was the familiar smell of the rundown casino. Old carpets and cigarette smoke and burnt popcorn.

Guys like Wendell with fancy titles who dressed like an executive to give the small-time casino the illusion of class. But it was the same old rundown bullshit Trucks had known all his life. He'd lived it again and again. A dream on repeat.

"Haven't eaten much lately. Just moved to town. I've been showing my girl the sights." Trucks pointed at Claudia with his thumb.

"She's adorable. Where'd you take her?"

"Around. So you got anything at middle, then?"

"I'd suggest cutting to lightweight, but if you're not eating much, it'd probably kill you."

The guy had a touch of sinister. Trucks didn't like it.

"Anything at middle?" Trucks repeated.

Wendell pulled a small notebook from his breast pocket. He flipped through some pages.

"Can you be ready in two days?"

"Sure."

"We had a guy from Babb pull out with a sinus infection. I can mark you down to replace him at middleweight."

"Okay."

"You sure you can be on that weight?"

"Yeah."

"What do I pencil you in as?"

Trucks thought a second.

"Kadoka," he said.

"All right."

Wendell put his notebook away.

"What's the pay?" Trucks asked.

"Forty dollars."

"Rounds?"

"Four."

"Ten bucks a round?"

"Look, math whiz, I don't know anything about you. You come in, fight hard, do good, we'll pay you more. For now, yeah. Undercard fight, ten bucks a round."

Trucks nodded. He looked over at Claudia. She was watching him. She looked desperate to know.

Trucks looked back to Wendell.

"Win bonus?" Trucks asked.

"Sometimes. Twenty bucks or so. Depends on the finish and quality."

"That's fair. Cash after?"

"Come find me."

"I appreciate you writing me in. We need this," Trucks said, almost pleading.

"Just remember, the event starts at seven. You'll go on third, unless the promoters flip the card. You're fighting a guy in his thirties out of Whitefish. A little washed up. You'll make good ringfellows, I'm sure. He's got a decent gas tank, a sharp hook."

"All right. Nothing new. Eaten a few of those in my life."

"I can see that."

"Any chance you can spot me the gloves and ring attire?"

Wendell laughed.

"Just checking," Trucks said.

"I get it. Believe me," Wendell said. "Hard times, right?"

Trucks picked the tote bag off the floor. The weight of all they had.

"Hard fucking times."

THE CLEAN AND THE GOOD

They say ring rust is real. And Trucks was feeling it that night. He'd lost all his wind from weeks of not training. He was taking a lot of damage. Blood ran from his nose to his upper lip. He hadn't landed anything clean in three rounds. They were about to start the fourth. Trucks was sitting on his stool in the corner.

The volunteer corner man talked to Trucks as he jammed cotton swabs up his nose. He needed to end the fight. Get the win bonus.

"You gonna make one more round?" the corner man said. "You're gassing out there."

Trucks nodded.

"You've been gassing the whole time."

"I'm gunning for him this time. Get the smelling salts ready."

The corner man snickered, clearly not buying it. He tossed the swabs in his bucket and gave Trucks a last drink of water. Then he popped Trucks's mouthpiece in. The one they'd given him when he showed up early at the casino. He'd had to boil the mold in a pot in the casino's kitchen and apply it to his teeth. And now it was earning its worth in punishment.

"Catch him if you got something to throw," the corner

man said. "Breathe, for fuck's sake."

Trucks stood.

The corner man took the stool.

Trucks adjusted his shorts. He alternated driving each foot into the mat. Looked down at his black wrestling shoes. Tied tight. Secondhand. The gloves and shorts and shoes. Everything lifted the day before.

Then the bell rang.

Trucks took the center of the ring. Both men were tired. Whitefish was carrying more muscle. Stocky. So he was losing oxygen faster trying to feed those muscles. Trucks let him get off a couple flush shots to the body. A few knocks to the head.

Trucks clenched with Whitefish and went limp. He made Whitefish carry all his weight. Let him bully Trucks into the corner and blast away. Trucks put up his gloves and felt the vibration of the blows along his arms. He was calculating it real smooth. Blocking most of the punches.

Trucks worked out of the corner and moved down the ropes. He felt the burn along his back. Whitefish followed him with heavy straights. Left hooks. He was getting tired chasing after Trucks.

Before Trucks got to the next turnbuckle, he pivoted and caught Whitefish with a short uppercut. *Pah.*

It stunned Whitefish.

Trucks rolled around and pushed Whitefish against the ropes. Then he got off a flurry—*pah-pah-pah-pah*. Everything to the body. When Whitefish dipped to protect his midsection, Trucks torqued his hips and launched a nasty left hook that connected with Whitefish's jaw. It was real stiff. The kind of shot that could lay a man clean out. The kind of shot that did.

Whitefish fell to the canvas. The ref ushered Trucks into a neutral corner. Whitefish got to a knee, took a heaving breath, and stood. He put his gloves out, fists together. The ref gave him the mandatory eight-count, grabbed his wrists, and asked if he wanted to continue. Whitefish nodded.

Trucks rushed forward, ready to kill.

And just in that movement, Whitefish came out of the haze and caught Trucks with an overhand right that wobbled him. A barrage followed. Trucks went blurry. Had he timed it wrong? Moved in too soon? Too reckless?

Before Trucks recovered, the bell sounded. Trucks and Whitefish hugged and raised each other's hands in a show of sportsmanship. Whitefish thumped Trucks on the chest, told him he'd caught him clean and with wicked power. Trucks said something back. He didn't know what. His temples were pounding. His mind in a fog.

The judges' scores were read as Whitefish and Trucks stood side by side. Trucks lost a unanimous decision on the cards. Whitefish raised his hands. Trucks looked for Claudia.

THE LETHARGY OF BULLSHIT

"There's twenty," Wendell said. He handed Trucks the bills. They were standing in a small alcove near the casino lobby.

Trucks eyed him with frustration. Wendell owed him forty. His hands shook as he counted the money, just in case Wendell had misspoke. Nope. Only twenty there. Trucks folded the bills and put them in his back pocket. He'd changed into his winter clothes for the long walk back. His gloves and shorts and wrestling shoes packed away. Claudia was silent beside him. Their tote bag on the ground.

"You were really going for that win bonus," Wendell said. "I like guys who dish it out like that. Excites the crowd. Creates buzz. Gets people charged about coming to the next event. Maybe next time don't wait for the last round to turn it on, huh?"

"Yeah," Trucks said. "Maybe."

He stared into the distance. Clenched his fists. His hands were swollen and red. His head still spinning. He didn't feel right. And now he was angry.

"Your boxing days over, or are you looking for more work?" Wendell asked. He pulled the notebook from his breast pocket. "Got another one here in a couple days."

Trucks looked at Claudia. She was tired and upset. There

was such a distance in her energy, like she was long gone away.

"Pepper Flake, you wanna get some candy from the machine over there?" Trucks pointed across the room. Then he worked through his pockets and pulled out a quarter. "Go get yourself some of that candy."

Claudia took the coin and walked away. She looked like a little zombie, out of heart.

Trucks turned back to Wendell.

"Nice parenting," Wendell said.

"Go fuck yourself," Trucks said.

Wendell smiled. "You'd have knocked him out if you used that kinda fire from the get-go."

"Where's my other twenty? You said ten dollars a round. Forty bucks."

Wendell smoothed a hand over one of his lapels.

"How would you score your activity in the first couple rounds?"

"Did all right."

"You were gassed in the first. Chugging in the second and third. You're lucky you got half. If it wasn't for your effort in the last round, you wouldn't have gotten shit."

The fire was burning in Trucks, all right. This man had no idea. If he wanted the storm-bringer, Trucks would oblige with fists like flame.

But then he thought about his girl. He couldn't settle matters that way anymore. It had to be about his girl. Only his girl. He repeated that in his broken mind until all he was hearing was *only* over and over. *Only. Only. Only.*

"So the job," Trucks finally said. He put a hand to his

temple and rubbed.

"Like I said, a couple days. From the looks of things, you can't go heavier than middle. I got one at super-welter. You think you can drop six pounds?"

Trucks looked over at Claudia. The little red candy machine had jammed. It was round and looked like a fat parking meter. She was hitting it with her palm.

"Yeah, I can drop the weight."

"All right. I'll mark you down for super-welter in two days. This guy's out of Chouteau. Don't worry, he's not French or anything, so he's going to give you a real fight." Wendell laughed at his own joke. Then he said, "Bring it from the first bell. He's younger and faster than you. You'll get your full pay when you earn it. Quit stepping in the lethargy of bullshit and bring it next time. Like your life depends on it."

Wendell walked off.

Trucks picked up the tote bag and went over to Claudia. His back muscles were already feeling sore from throwing all those punches. He hadn't truly thrown any for a while. The few shots he'd popped off at the shelter didn't count. And his head. It hurt so bad.

Trucks walked up to Claudia. She sat cross-legged on the ground in front of the machine.

"It's broke," she said.

"Well, don't give up on it. I'm sure we can get the candy out."

"I don't want the candy. I wanna go home."

He hated to hear that word. He didn't know anymore what her use of it would mean. Like a weapon she wielded over him.

Trucks set down the tote bag. He turned the little metal lever on the machine, and the quarter spit out. He put it in his pocket. Then he held out his hand. Claudia sighed, reached up, and he pulled her to her feet. She stood there resigned as he made sure her hearing aids were snug, adjusted her headband over her ears, pulled her hood on, buttoned the throat flaps of her coat, and stood. Trucks grabbed the tote bag from the ground. He wanted to carry it to save her any burden.

They stopped at the glass exit doors in the casino lobby. Gathering as much warmth as they could before they made their march.

"It'll get easier, Clarinda. You can count on that," he said.

He'd called her the wrong name but didn't realize it. His mind rattled and coming apart. Claudia heard it but didn't know what it meant. His words had become like a fog ever fading. Too many promises. Too many speeches. His words meant little now.

They stared at the windows. Their soft reflections against the harsh streetlights beyond. Snow blowing outside like pale confetti floating across the landscape.

"Trust me," he said. But he didn't know if he was saying it to her or trying to comfort himself about their long road ahead. Not just the walk through the cold. The dark. Maybe it was about their difficult walk of life together. But wasn't it that word—*together*—that made even the harsh feel beautiful? He was glad more than anything to have her. And then he told her. He said it outright. The fire burning in his faded mind and sloping body.

Time passed. It was slow. Or it was fast. He couldn't tell. Then Claudia grabbed his wrist. A touch he'd keep eternal.

His mind stormed with all the shots he'd taken. It was more disorienting than it had ever been. He couldn't shake off the haze like in years past. And the boxing just didn't feel the same.

When she let go they launched forward. Pushed through the doors and trudged on. Their breaths flowing behind them like smokestacks. The licks of the night fresh on their cold faces.

AN IMPOSSIBLE PENDULUM

He wasn't eating. He had to drop the weight.

Trucks had awoken several times in the night with intense headaches. He'd tried hard not to disturb Claudia, but he'd seize awake. Whether it was from a nightmare or pain, he didn't know. But he'd shake awake, and sometimes it'd disrupt her sleep. As if the wind wasn't enough. The groaning boards. That incessant nighttime howling from so far away.

Trucks bought her gas station pancakes again. He might have been screwed out of the other twenty dollars Wendell owed him, but the money he had given Trucks really meant something. It wasn't enough to get them much, but it was a start.

They sat at the same table by the window. Trucks watched Claudia eat. Sometimes he stared at the fuel pumps. Fingerprints all over the window to the outside world. He was looking at those fuel pumps now. So isolated. So stuck. Rooted to that unforgiving cement foothold.

"You better finish those, Clarinda," he said. "You need your strength after all the walking." Trucks was still staring out the window.

"Stop calling me that!" Claudia said.

Trucks turned to her.

"What?"

"You keep calling me Cluhrinna."

"I do?"

"You said *Cluhrinna*. You called me that again."

"Clarinda?"

"Stop, I hate hearing it!"

Claudia dropped her plastic fork and covered her ears.

"I called you that? When?"

Claudia uncuffed her ears.

"When? When did I say that?"

"Last night when you said to watch for cars."

Trucks closed his eyes. He tried to think. He felt a constant dull headache. Like a dying radio wave.

"I did?"

She nodded. "And after we brushed our teeth. You made us do it twice."

"Twice? Why?"

Claudia shrugged.

"And I called you Clar—that name?"

"Yeah, and I don't like it. I really don't like it."

Trucks was baffled. He didn't recall it last night or this morning. Even now he remembered saying her name, but hadn't he said *Claudia*? But he never called her that. Why would he start now?

"Pepper Flake," he said, like he'd just remembered. "You're my little pepper flake."

Claudia was agitated. She took her fork and cut her smooshed pancakes into ever-smaller pieces.

Trucks looked out the window again. A shiny red jeep pulled up to the pump. A pretty blonde stepped out and rubbed her hands together. He thought of June. He wondered about her. How she was getting on in South Dakota. He felt so guilty for messing up at the shelter. For causing Claudia to lose June's scent. And Gerald's gambling token too. All the special things they'd gathered. Gone in one shot.

"How about we head back to that big old library again? Remember how it looked like a spaceship inside? That crazy ceiling. All the colors. We could grab some books and read. It's warm in there. We'd have to hide from the front desk, but I'm sure they wouldn't notice. And maybe it wouldn't really matter. Maybe the shelter never told them about what happened."

Claudia stabbed her pancake.

"Think it over while you're finishing breakfast. It's really our only free day before the next match, and I want it to be good for you."

"Fight," she said. "It's a stupid, stupid fight. And they already hit you so hard they messed up your bruiseity brains."

"Hey, I'm all right. Just a little headache."

"They're falling out. I knew it would happen. I told you!"

"Hey, calm down. It's okay."

Trucks got up and sat beside her.

Claudia scooted toward the glass. She put her arms on the table and put her face on them.

Trucks looked down at her chopped-apart pancakes.

"It's not okay," Claudia said into her arms. "Your bruiseity brains. I told you. I told you."

Trucks wanted to rub her back. Comfort her. But she was so sensitive about his touches now. He didn't want to make it worse. He always felt stuck between loving her and hurting her. An impossible pendulum.

"It's still me. It's always me," he said. "Pepper Flake. See? I said it right. I said it again."

Claudia cried. Everything had been taken out of her. From her.

"I'll get better. The headache's gonna go away. I'll quit calling you the wrong name. I promise. It'll get better. It has to get better. A few more fights and we're on our way to our own little apartment where you can have a room. Your own space. You can do whatever you want in there. Build forts and color and put puzzles together. We're really on our way. Just a few more matches. A couple good paydays. A knockout here and there. A handful of Ws. Some win-bonus money. You'll see. Have faith. Isn't that what they're always saying? A few more good matches, and we're really on our way. We are."

Trucks scooted closer. He didn't know what else to say. Sometimes his words meant nothing at all. He rested his head on her shoulder and felt the vibrations of her crying. The heaves of her small body. All the breath she could muster. All the heart she had left.

TAKING IT TO CHOUTEAU

He started out faster. Nearly ran to the center of the ring. Took control of the space. He'd starved himself and lost the six pounds. Trucks knew it wouldn't be long before he gassed. His head was still throbbing, but the adrenaline dump masked the pain.

Trucks tried to keep Chouteau off with quick jabs, but like Wendell said, he was younger and quicker. Chouteau parried the jabs or slipped off to the side. He threw counter hooks to Trucks's head when he slipped in, right crosses when he slipped out.

Trucks pulled Chouteau into the clinch. He could hear Chouteau talking to him, but with the beating in his head and the blur of combat and heavy breaths, he couldn't make out the words.

The ref broke the clinch.

Trucks clipped Chouteau with a left hook on the break. He didn't get him clean but realized the younger fighter didn't protect on the break. Something to remember.

Trucks maintained the center of the ring. He kept Chouteau on his heels heading back to the ropes. Chouteau fired heavy straights and uppercuts but often missed. His form was rough, his punches sloppy.

Each time Trucks jabbed to set up a right cross, Chouteau would cleverly bob, weave, slip, or parry the punches. His defense was excellent. It was strange he had such a gap of defense during and after the clinch. Trucks could tell he wasn't used to dirty boxing. Probably trained in a softer-style club where they only taught the clean stuff. Trucks had learned it rough, battling other kids from the homes and on the streets for years.

He used that knowledge to pick Chouteau apart up close. Trucks threw looping hooks and long jabs into Chouteau's face. Even when Chouteau parried or evaded, Trucks would stick to him. Wouldn't let up. Chase him down like a rabid beast.

Pah-pah-pah-pah.

When he got close, Trucks would pull Chouteau in and throw heavy body shots. Hit him with uppercuts. Rough him up with his shoulder when they were tight together.

Time was ticking. Maybe a minute left in the round. Trucks was tired. His wind was really sucked out. He was breathing through his mouth and having trouble keeping his hands up. Chouteau caught him a few times between the gloves, around the gloves, through the gloves.

More blasts to his damaged brain. The rattling wore on.

Out of desperation, Trucks threw a stiff overhand right that knocked Chouteau into the ropes. Trucks followed up by wrapping Chouteau in a bear hug and squeezing hard. He dug his chin into Chouteau's trapezius muscle and knocked heads with him. Anything to mess with the kid's mind and keep him uncomfortable.

When the ref stepped in to break the clinch, he admonished Trucks.

Trucks still had Chouteau near the ropes and stepped back into the pocket. He threw several feints to the head and body. Got Chouteau thinking. Then Trucks initiated another clinch and blasted away. This time he didn't wait for the ref to step in. Instead, Trucks broke the clinch himself, faked a step back, and caught Chouteau with an unexpected gazelle hook.

Chouteau stumbled back. He let all the weight of him go against the ropes, and Trucks moved in. His eyes full of fire. No thought in his mind. Only the pure, brutal instincts of a man on the edge, protecting the small, precious life he'd worked so hard to make.

A blur of fists on the wobbly fish against the ropes. All those unharmonious thuds. The ref pulling Trucks off. Waving his arms overhead. Calling the fight.

Trucks walked away weary. The smell of hot-iron blood in his nose. Down his throat. The blur of the ring and the crowd and all those angled lights.

He stumbled across the canvas, tasting the blood. Trucks rested his forearms on the coiled top rope. The sweat rolling off him. He looked out to see his girl in the back row. She wasn't even looking his way. Had her back to the ring. Probably hadn't watched a second of it.

Trucks stood there. Hopeless. Leaning. Trying to think. A buzz in his mind. A sharp pulsing.

The volunteer corner man came over and wiped around Trucks's face and neck. Trucks leaned on the ropes with all he had left. Hoping his girl might look over. See what he'd accomplished. What he'd done for them. That he'd bested another man in battle. And was there anything harder than that? Anything that took more guts and courage? Anything to be prouder about? Year after year reaching down into the utter pit of himself and pulling something out to save them. This drive from the rarest of all deep places. Like a magician who could just pluck it right out. As if from the depths of some unknown inner pocket.

THE SONIC EMBRYO

He took her hand as they cut through the dark. His mind was fading, and he could feel it. Sense it disintegrating under the weight of the blows. All those years of knuckle on bone. The knocks. Compounded into the sharp flares and pulses. *Thwup-Thwup*. His head hurt like that. *Thwup*.

Claudia pulled her hand away. Not quick. Not angry. Just slow and careful. Almost sedate.

Their breaths puffed out as they crunched along. The hard-packed snow under their boots.

Trucks didn't know if they'd said anything to each other since leaving the casino. He remembered nothing but flashes after he stepped down from the ring. The scissors gliding through his white knuckle tape. A couple tabs of aspirin on his palm. Him and the boys used to call it Sally Ace. The little white pills made of salicylic acid.

"Give me some of that Sally Ace," Trucks said out into the cold.

Claudia looked up at him. Didn't say anything back.

"I love you," Trucks said. "I don't really say that, huh?"

Claudia stayed silent. They kept walking. The tote bag swung from Trucks's wrist.

"Well, I do. I guess I should say it more. Nobody ever said stuff like that to me. So I—" He felt a sharp sting in his temple. "So I should work on that. I'll remember."

It felt colder that night. Even without the whipping wind. There was a pure chill out there. The Billings streets near empty. The errant flickers of the dying streetlights. The two of them moving stiff in the dark.

"I just wanted you to know I love you. I hope it means something."

He looked down at her as they walked. Her face was pink. She had her hands jammed in her coat pockets. He was hoping those oversized gloves were still doing the trick.

"It's okay if you don't have anything to say about that. Because you know I'm trying. And trying means a whole lot where we come from."

They continued in silence. Whenever a car passed, Trucks would watch the eyes of the driver. Looks of pity that ate him up.

Another sharp pain in his temple. He breathed in hard through his mouth. His nose was swollen and full of dried blood.

A few minutes later, Trucks heard what sounded like a snap of thunder. Saw a streak up in the sky. Golden bright with a pink layer in the middle. Like a sonic embryo shooting across the universe.

"Holy shit," he said, and stopped walking.

Claudia stopped too.

"What?" she said.

Trucks put a hand to his head and rubbed his temple.

"What?" she said. "What?"

"Did you see that?" he said.

Trucks dropped the tote bag and scooped up Claudia. He

set her on top of a bus stop bench along the road.

"Look at the sky. Look out there," he said.

"At what?"

"I don't know. But look. It's moving so fast. That bright streak. There it goes, see?"

Trucks leaned against her body. Stuck his arm out at an upward angle and pointed his shaky left hand at the black sky.

"I can't see it. Where? Where?" she said.

"Right there. There!"

"Where?"

"The bright light. The streak. It's golden and beautiful. Can't you see it? Look. Look, for fuck's sake!"

"I'm trying. It's not there. I can't see it. I don't see anything!"

Trucks's head throbbed. It was so sharp and severe. But he kept pointing.

"It's going right to left. Coming down at an angle. Follow my hand."

She followed his hand.

"It's lighting up the sky out there. Going faster. Faster."

"I can't see it. It's not there! Nothing's there!"

"Are you following my finger?"

"Yes!"

"Dammit. But it's so bright."

"Dammit," she said.

"How can you not see it? It's just so damn bright," he said.

"I don't know. I don't know!" she said.

"Oh no," he said.

"What?"

"It's fading. It's getting too far. Can't you see it yet?"

"No. I can't. I wanna see. Where? Tell me where!"

"There! Keep following my finger. Just look. Quick. Hurry. I think it's fading. It's going out."

"I don't see it! There's nothing there. Only dark."

"No, it's got a little light left. Here."

He hooked his arm around her waist and pulled her tight to him. Their heads were touching. His throbbing and hers so cold.

"There, Clarinda. It's so there," he said.

And then he closed his eyes and pointed as hard as he could into the night.

UNDER THE ARCHES

They washed in the morning. Wiped themselves with harsh paper towels and hand soap. It was always cold in the cement-walled bathroom hut. Trucks had hoped it would shock his mind back to normal. But he knew something was really off now. His brainwaves perpetually on the verge of short circuit.

After they were clean and dry, Trucks rolled up the mummy bag and put it in the stuff sack. He loaded the tote bag for the morning walk to the gas station.

Claudia sat at the picnic table. She bit into the fingers of her glove.

Trucks thought of the sixty dollars he'd earned last night. Tucked in his back pocket. Forty for the work, twenty for the win bonus. It put them around seventy-six dollars. They were on their way. He'd only remembered the previous night in flashes. Wendell's smug face. The bills placed in his hand. Wendell mentioning two days. Their last big promotion for a while. Wanted Trucks to fight a kid from, shit, had he said Kalispell? Anyway, the kid from Kalispell had stiff jabs. Better watch out. So said Wendell in flashes.

Trucks left the tote bag and sat across from Claudia at the picnic table. His head hurt, but he didn't let on.

"How's your back and side?" he asked. "Still a little sore

from the hard wood?"

Claudia didn't answer. Sleeping on the picnic table wasn't easy. But it was the howling that really got to Trucks.

In front of them was the small sweeping city. They could see it all from up there in the park. The few tall buildings, dark against the white snow. An army of bare trees. The ridges of the rugged land all around. There was little sun that morning. Just rays peeking through. The rest a gray filter around them.

"Soon it can be regular. Not just pancakes. We'll have fruit and cereal and the good bread. Not that white cardboard."

Claudia sighed.

"What?" he said.

"You always say stuff like that."

"What should I say?"

"I don't know. Something true."

"Why wouldn't that be true?"

Claudia rested her chin on the table.

"Isn't that cold?"

She didn't answer.

"Why wouldn't that be true?" A pain in his head. "Couldn't it be true?"

"You imagine it. Like lives you talk about. You tell me it'll be nicer, but it's never nicer. It's freezing. And it just gets worse. It's okay eating pancakes. I don't care. I just want a place where people are nice to me and it's warm and kids don't make fun of my hearing phones."

"But nobody's made fun of you," he said. He felt a catch in his throat.

"That's 'cause I'm only around you. Not other kids. But they'd probably just make fun of me and call me names 'cause of my hearing phones." She reached up and touched them. "It makes me weird."

"We're not all the same," Trucks said. "And we don't have to be. It's okay you don't hear so good. And maybe in the future when I get us more money we can buy you some hearing ai—phones that fit good and people won't even be able to notice. Maybe we can find some as small as little bees."

Claudia looked out at the city. Trucks did the same. They sat looking under the arches of the wooden gazebo. A slight wind blowing through.

"Maybe we should get inside somewhere warm," he said.

Claudia ignored him.

"Do you really think I'm lying about the lives? You think I don't mean it when I say it'll be better? That I can bring us better? Don't you believe in me?"

Claudia didn't answer.

"I guess we should get down to the gas station, then," he said. "We wait too long and the pancakes aren't on special."

Trucks stood and made sure everything was in the tote bag. His ears were ringing. A thrumming pinch in his brain.

When he looked up, Claudia was already down the path. But he hadn't been sifting through the bags that long, had he? It made his heart ache to see her so far away. He hooked the tote-bag straps around his wrist and ran after her. Each hurried footfall forcing the small speck of her ever closer.

THE HOWLS OF DEVASTATION

You suffocate everything you love.
Trucks shot up in the dark. Claudia stirred. She made a noise, twisted in the bag, and went back to sleep. Trucks lay awake. Wide-eyed. Sweating, yet cold. He stared through the face hole of the mummy bag and gripped the internal zipper with his fingers. He squeezed it tight.

Who had said that to him? It must have been one of the free-clinic therapists from so many years ago.

His head ached. He bit down and flexed his muscles to ward off the pain. Nothing helped. Sometimes it came in pulses. Like red blinks of pain. Other times it lasted and lasted. Seeming endless. A torture earned.

His thoughts ran. Was that what he always did? Suffocated everyone and everything he loved? Pulled them in and squeezed too hard from the fear of losing them if he let go? Did he know how to do it any other way? Could he ever learn different?

And Claudia. Breathing deeply against him in what felt like tranquil sleep. He hoped she was dreaming of other worlds. Other universes. Places so far beyond what they'd known and what he could give her that she might even forget it altogether.

"I'm a fuck-up," he whispered to her. "I'm so sorry for

being such a fuck-up."

Trucks gasped. He felt the warm tears rolling down his cheeks. He let go of the zipper and covered his mouth. His body convulsed. The harsh movements of such deep sadness.

He unzipped the bag, got out, and zipped it back up. He put on his boots and walked partway down the hill against the harsh wind. It was so damn cold. He pulled on his hood and stuck his hands in his coat pockets.

Trucks sat in the snow. The tears still rolling. He was shaking. He was sad.

"You're such a fuck-up, you're such a fuck-up," he said. And he didn't stop. He kept repeating it. His body shivering. The tears coming. His head throbbing.

He took his hands out of his pockets and hit himself in the side of the head.

"Work, goddamn you. Work!"

But all he could do was sob across the big hill. The glowing lights of the city so bright below. Twinkling orange and yellow. Like he was looking at an inverted buzz of constellations he'd never know.

The realization made him angry. With the unforgiving world. With his past. With his inabilities. With the fucked up parts of himself.

He hit himself again and again. Berating himself for crying. For his weaknesses. For his inability to keep it together. To give his girl the life she deserved.

And with every blow he spoke in spit and tears. Trying to convince himself of something he was no longer sure of.

"I'm not a beast. I'm not a beast. I'm not a beast."

Anything near that hill would have heard the sounds of

his breaking. But it wouldn't have sounded like a man. The loud shiver of sobs from so deep within that broken spirit. They'd have resonated more like the howls of devastation. The hurt of an uncharted species.

THE CALLING DARKNESS

A right hook caught him off guard and sent him to the ropes. Trucks covered and dipped down. The kid threw everything stiff. It wasn't just his jabs.

The shots landed harsh on his body. He could feel the ricochets off his gloves and forearms as he covered up. The taut coil of the ropes against his back. He was trying to survive. Seeing blinks of light like electric shocks. *Pop-pop.* The thud of the oncoming punches. The vibrations all over his body.

It was nothing but survival. Make the bell. Let the round be over.

But Trucks dug deep. He was guts and grit and hard-beaten man. He pushed the kid away and came off the ropes. Caught him in the center of the ring with a jumping hook to the temple. The kid shook it off and plodded forward. Trucks tied him up in the clinch to stall. Blood from a cut above his eye waved down the kid's back. Trucks watched the little trail of blood. He held on tight.

The ref stepped in and broke up the clinch. On the exit, the kid hit a nice uppercut and wobbled Trucks just before the bell.

Trucks staggered toward his corner. When he started going the wrong way, the ref righted him. The volunteer corner man put the stool down from the outside. Then he came through the ropes with his bucket of supplies and met Trucks in the corner.

Trucks sat on the stool. He was two rounds deep and feeling every second of it. The third was coming on like a wildfire. He was weary and wobbly. His head was spinning. The room was quaking. He blinked rapidly and shook his head hard to clear his eyes of sweat and blood.

The corner man pulled his mouthpiece out and threw it in the bucket. Fed water to him. Then he capped the water bottle and rolled a thick cotton swab across the cut over Trucks's eye. He pressed hard with his thumb. Then he switched to the eye iron and pressed it on a hematoma forming on Trucks's right temple.

"What's happening out there?" the corner man said. "You look god-awful. You okay to go back out? You look like you're on Dream Street."

Trucks nodded.

"You keep eating shots like that, I'm calling it."

Trucks nodded again.

"Keep away from his jab. Find a better range and slip under. Pop him with that left hook you're supposed to have."

The corner man sealed the gash with salve mixed with epinephrine. Then he popped the mouthpiece back in. Trucks stood. The corner man snatched the stool and hopped out of the ring.

Ding.

Trucks turned with a new urgency. He rushed forward. Took the center of the ring. He feinted on some jabs, then started throwing wild power combinations. Hooks, uppercuts, haymakers. It wasn't technical.

The kid backed off. Surprised. But he patiently pedaled the outside. Kept working that jab to create space.

"Come on, you fuck," Trucks said through all the throbbing. "That all you brought from Kasper?"

Trucks could feel the beast inside him rising. He edged closer. He pulled the kid into a clinch and started throwing to the body. *Pah-pah-pah.* The kid didn't like it. This knowing burned in Trucks's guts. Told him: chase the beacon of weakness.

The ref stepped in and split them apart.

Trucks pursued with all the bull heat he had left. He backed the kid up with his wild combinations, whiffing many, catching the kid's gloves on a few. But soon he had the kid in the corner and was throwing all he had left into his shots. Head to body and back. *Pah-pah-pah-pah.* They were stiff and hard and angry. Like he wanted to end this kid.

But the kid was young and tough. Resilient. And Trucks was exhausted. He barely had any wind coming into the fight. He was frail and tired and blowing out all his fuses.

The kid was smart. He had energy. He absorbed the punches like a patient sparrow. Waited for the second when Trucks let up, then the kid spun off the ropes with a shove. Instead of retreating, the kid stepped back into the pocket. Threw two quick, stiff jabs followed by a wicked uppercut. So harsh and fast and powerful, like he'd pulled it up from his toes.

Trucks's head snapped back. He saw a shock of white. Then he buckled and dropped to a knee. Grasped the rope with that trusty left. But nothing could hold him then, and everything gave in that moment.

The ref moved the kid into a neutral corner and came over to work the standing eight-count. But it was clear Trucks was done. He was wobbly even on a knee and wouldn't be getting up. His eyes were glazed over, his head drooping. The ref waved off the fight.

Trucks slid to the ground. He laid there for a while, watching the tiny air particles float against the hot lights above. The dull roar of the crowd. Trucks stared into the calling darkness behind all that harsh light. Stared and stared. Like a madman. Or someone who'd lost something from the deepest part of the soul.

The next thing he knew he was sitting up, the ref waving smelling salts under his nose. A few men clutching him under the armpits and dragging him out of the ring and down the steel steps. On instinct, Trucks babbled, "Take me to my girl, my girl," but they didn't know what that meant.

They sat him down in a chair at the back of the room. A doctor shined a light in his eyes and asked him questions about his consciousness. Ran fingers through his field of vision.

Count it like a kid.

How many? How many? How many?

Five. Three. One. Three. Four.

A person from the medical staff came. She sewed the cut above his eye. Quick pulls and snips. And soon he was alone.

They'd given him a bottle of water. It rolled at his feet. His black wrestling shoes askew. He knew he'd needed to remember something, but he couldn't recall what. To think anything was hard. To collect himself, nearly impossible. The room shifted. They'd stripped him of the gloves and cut the knuckle tape from his hands. But when had they done that? His hands were red. This time not from the cold. Red from the sweat. The heat. The pounding. The brutal bashing of knuckles under leather. *Pah-pah.*

His girl. It hit him. He stood to reach for her. Then the thought was gone.

He swayed under the lights. An announcer roared over a tinny PA system.

Trucks sat down. He leaned back in the steel chair and closed his eyes. Just to sleep. Just a little bit. Not too long. Only a while. Just to sleep. Only to sleep. Only.

UNDER A FLURRY

Trucks woke in the mummy bag. He was drenched in sweat. Claudia tight against him. They were bundled in their winter clothes. It felt like they were steaming in the bag. His head was killing him. He didn't remember anything after falling asleep in the chair after the fight.

Trucks looked through the face hole. It was dark out. The gazebo arches whined above. Trucks unzipped the bag and started to get out. He tried to do it gently to avoid waking her. Claudia shifted as he slid out from under her. She mumbled in her sleep.

"I'll be back, Clarinda," he whispered.

Trucks got out of the bag and zipped it up. He put on his boots and walked through the night to the bathroom hut. He turned on the light and went to the sink. Trucks looked in the mirror. His face was all kinds of fucked up. His eyes red. The right temple swollen and purple and aching. He touched the stitched cut on his forehead. The skin itched around where she'd done the sewing. It always did. He wanted to tear out the stitches.

Trucks turned on the faucet and leaned down to splash water on his face. His back hurt from the bending, the muscles sore from all the punches he'd thrown.

He put his hands under the running water. Watched

them fill up and tried desperately to remember something from after the fight as he looked into the small pool in his palms. How had he found Claudia? How did they get back to the gazebo? Did he feed her? Was she okay? What did they talk about, if anything, on the way back?

Endless questions ran through his mind. He watched the water run over his swollen hands. He threw more water on his face, then dried himself with paper towels.

Trucks gripped the sink and stared into the mirror. He looked so hard and long that he eventually didn't recognize who was looking back at him. Staring at a ghost of himself. Some alternate-universe version. He was old. Beat up. Out of energy. Out of place. Out of time.

"Who the fuck are you?" he said.

No answer.

"The world is brutal," he said.

No answer.

That wasn't him in the mirror.

Trucks closed his eyes. He rubbed them hard. He saw bright sparks shoot across his closed-eyed darkness.

He opened his eyes. The sparks flew for a while against the light, then it was all normal again. As normal as his life could be now.

He wondered then if he'd ever kill himself. Not with his girl around. Never then. But he wondered still. And if he was going to die, he'd want to die in the ring under a flurry of punches. It had happened before. To other men. It could happen again. It was the weight of that risk that drew people like him into the ring. Always walking out on some kind of jagged ledge. Never knowing how long the earth of the cliff could hold.

He had an urge to check his pockets. There were bloody tissues in his coat. He threw them in the trash. In his back pocket he found a few bills. He unfolded them. There was less money now than when he'd gone to the fight. Had he been robbed?

Trucks folded the bills and put them in his back pocket. He was woozy and confused.

The overhead light flickered. Trucks was brought back to the pulsing pain in his body. His head throbbed. He rubbed his temples. Nothing helped.

Trucks shut the light off and left the bathroom hut. He made his way to the gazebo. He looked at the mummy bag on the table under the arches. Like his girl was coffined in that sleek pouch. It twisted his stomach. Like he could vomit. The thought of her dead. Gone.

He looked up at the night sky. The moon was hidden. Stolen under clouds or simply tucked behind a dark universe he'd never comprehend.

Trucks smelled his hands. The scent of dirty money.

He felt a rush of panic. He didn't know why. Trucks ran over to the tote bag he must have tied to the loop on the outside of the mummy bag. He dug through the bags until he found his sachet of antibacterial wipes. He sat on the bench and scrubbed his hands. Then he threw the wipe on the ground. Grabbed another. He took off his coat and rolled up his sweatshirt sleeves. Scrubbed up and down his arms. Two. Three. Four wipes. He threw them on the ground. Then he took off his sweatshirt. It was so cold. He ached as he grabbed wipe after wipe. Gritted his teeth against the frigid night and fiercely brushed his body. He felt the burn of the scrubbing and the alcohol. The chill of the wind. Soon he was down to nothing. Naked and freezing. A pile of wipes at his feet as he jumped in the cold. Rubbing his numb skin so hard that it felt like he was scraping it off. The whipping wind. The wipes like sandpaper. Himself disappearing with each harsh scrub.

When he was numb and red, he put on his clothes and got in the bag. Trucks held Claudia and zipped them in. He was a shivering mess. Was he even a man anymore? A boxer? A father? He wasn't sure he could recognize himself. He didn't know if he ever would again.

Outside the mummy bag, he thought he heard a howling in the distance. Trucks could barely hear it over his chattering teeth. The noises a man makes at the bow of his breaking.

He felt one of Claudia's hearing aids claw against his cheek. He only held her tighter. Shut his eyes. Felt the warm sting of this rough life he'd carved as the litter of wipes outside were picked from the ground and scattered by the wind.

LIVING OFF INSTINCT

They were down to eighteen dollars. Trucks didn't know where the money had gone. He should have had over a hundred dollars after the fight. He'd probably been robbed in his delirium. He couldn't figure it any other way. He was pissed beyond belief. But he had to keep it buried to not upset Claudia any further. His head was no better. Everything in his mind was foggy. He was living off instinct.

He'd gotten her gas station pancakes. They sat at their usual table. Claudia hadn't said anything to him that morning. She was upset. He didn't know why.

"They good?" he asked about the pancakes.

Claudia chewed. She had anger in her eyes. He'd seen it before. He carried it too.

Trucks rubbed his temples. He pushed his fingers hard against them and released. It was punishing, but so was the pain.

"I was out of it last night. I'm sorry I don't remember anything."

Silence.

"Can you tell me what I did?"

Claudia cut her pancakes into the tiniest pieces.

"Please? I took some real heavy shots. You maybe saw it."

Trucks reached out, but Claudia pulled back. He looked

out the finger-printed window. Still not cleaned. Probably never would be.

"You keep calling me Cluhrinna," she said.

Trucks turned to her. His back was so sore.

"I'm sorry," he said.

"I hate that name. I *hate* it. I told you don't call me that."

"I'm really sorry. I was blacked out. I didn't even know."

"Your brains," she said. And then she went silent.

"My brains," he said.

They didn't talk for a while. Claudia ate more of her pancakes. She did it slow. Like it was a painful thing.

Trucks felt incapable. Weak. Like no part of him was sound. He'd never felt so inadequate. So unable to provide.

"I'm sorry," he said again. He just didn't know what to say anymore. Like he had no words.

Claudia was a wreck too. Tired eyes. Sallow skin. Her once-curly hair now frizzy and rough.

He'd failed her. There was nothing more to say than that. So he did.

"I failed you."

Claudia didn't say anything.

Trucks wavered between a sound and afflicted mind. The head trauma and despair pushing him ever closer to that faulty edge.

He looked out the window again. The blonde from days before pulled her red jeep up near the glass. She parked and walked in to buy cigarettes. She looked so much like June that it twisted his stomach. Trucks was transfixed on her. His head pounding. Then the smallest of ideas came to him in a flash. Or maybe it wasn't so small. Maybe it would utterly change their life.

"I'll be right back," he said.

Trucks stood. He swayed for a moment. Then he righted himself and walked along the small aisles. The cashier was distracted chatting with the pretty blonde. Probably lost in those glacier blue eyes. Trucks swiped a bottle of nighttime cold medicine and walked back to the table.

"I know you're mad at me," he said, sitting down, "but I've got something to make up for last night."

Claudia looked up from her plate. She tapped her plastic fork on the table.

"It's a new purp—"A bolt of pain shot through his head. He closed his eyes and tried to concentrate. "A new purple drink for kids. Supposed to give you lots of energy and make you run faster and jump higher and things. I read about it in a magazine."

Trucks opened his eyes. He tore apart the packaging under the table and hid the remains in his coat pocket. Then he pulled off the plastic covering. Unscrewed the lid. Tore off the safety seal. He worked swiftly with his hands.

"Drink your water down a bit," he said. "Get it about half."

Claudia looked suspicious.

"Go on," he said. "Trust me."

Claudia picked up her water cup and drank it down to half. Trucks saw movement at the window. The pretty blonde got into her car with the pack of cigarettes tight in her fist. She backed out and took off.

Trucks put the bottle on the table, the grip of his hand covering the label.

He poured a little syrup into the water. It changed to a soft purple.

"See the color?" he said.

She grabbed for the cup.

"Not yet," he said.

Claudia sat back, annoyed. She crossed her arms.

"It's sweet and tastes really good. They just came out with it, so most kids never tried it before. You're one of the first. Isn't that neat?" His head was pounding. He breathed in deep to handle it. "Okay, so here's the thing. You've gotta drink it all and drink it fast for it to work right. So you get all the vitamins."

Trucks poured a good portion of the bottle into the cup.

"Okay," he said.

Claudia picked up the cup. She smelled it.

"I like how it smells," she said.

He was going to right everything. He'd do it this time. It would work. No matter what he had to do or how he had to do it. It was time.

Claudia took a drink. Then another. She breathed between each one. After several attempts, she'd finished it.

"Wow," she said.

"Yeah," he said.

She sat back and held her stomach.

"It kinda hurts," she said.

"It's just the vitamins. Your stomach isn't used to it yet, but you'll see. You'll be so powerful. Not like me. You won't have these bruised brains falling out."

"Bruiseity brains," she said. "It's *bruiseity*."

"Right," he said. "It is."

AN OPENING

She slept so hard she almost seemed dead. That pale skin. Her soft eyelids.

An hour had passed. The headaches came and went. Sharper. Duller. More painful. Less painful. Always present. Trucks had stolen a loaf of bread, a jar of peanut butter, bottles of water, and another bottle of nighttime cold medicine, just in case. He had the tote bag packed and ready. He'd cleaned up their table. A new cashier had swapped out for the old one.

Finally, he saw what he was looking for. A guy had topped up his tires at the air hose, then filled his gas tank, then driven up to the side of the building. He parked away from the main windows and left his little car running.

This was it.

Trucks hooked the tote bag on one arm. He stood and picked Claudia out of her chair. It hurt his back, but he gritted his teeth. She had her sleepy head on his shoulder.

The guy came in and walked over to the cooler. Trucks made his way out the door and along the side of the gas station. The hum of the small running car, like the sound of liberation.

Trucks looked over his shoulder. Nobody in the lot was paying attention. He opened the driver's-side door and set

Claudia in the seat. He threw the tote bag in the back. Then he reached across her and unlocked the passenger door. He picked her up out of the seat and quickly carried her around the car. Trucks opened the passenger-side door, set her in the seat, and buckled her in. When he closed the door, he looked over the roof. Still, nothing. He ran around the car. With each footfall, his head pounded. Trucks opened the driver's-side door and got in. He put the car in gear, reversed, and took off like a bullet.

THE GREATEST DARK

Trucks flew down 90. Heading east. He could feel the tides of wind against the little car. Like it might blow them right off the road. But he kept the pedal pressed, his head down, always moving forward. A strategy he'd used so many times in that old ring.

Trucks often looked over at Claudia. Breathing deep. Sleeping hard. Sometimes he'd reach over and feel her chest rise, just to be sure.

He wondered if it was wrong. This deception. A sick magic act. But with all his failures he felt it had come down to this. A man doing all he could to save his girl from himself. To give her the best life he thought possible. A sad gift. The last attempt of a broken man.

When he saw the sign for Crow Agency, he felt a catch in his throat.

Trucks waved a hand against the cold glass. He pressed on.

The cities flew by like memories—Garryowen, Lodge Grass, Saddlestring. As the hours ticked by, the scenery seemed to blur at a denser rate. He'd rub his eyes, look at his girl, look back to the ever-smearing road. Delirium. Exhaustion. Near-collapse.

Somehow he kept his eyes open. His hands on the wheel. He clenched his jaw. Opened and closed his mouth. His sore back pressed against the seat. Sometimes he'd crank down the window and let the frigid air wake him. Seal it back up so he didn't freeze out his girl. He'd grip hard and go on.

He couldn't cover all that ground in a day. Or maybe he could. He didn't know how far it was, really. He just knew to stay on 90. Go east. Always east. A giant pewter horse in the yard. Jack Rose. Was it street? Lane? Avenue? It didn't matter. Couldn't be many of those out there. He'd find it. The horse his distant beacon. A landmark of new hope.

Along the way he decided he needed to write a letter. He couldn't just do this without some explanation. Trucks saw a big machine shed off an exit ramp near Sundance. He hit the brakes and took the exit. His girl thrust forward, stopped by the belt, and fell back in the seat. Trucks drove behind the machine shed and parked the car. He kept the engine running so the heat would stay on. Not for him. He was fine enough. It was for his sleeping girl.

His temples throbbed as he looked through the windshield. The sun was falling fast. It'd be dark soon. He knew that. Any fool would.

Trucks searched the car for paper. The visors, the glovebox, the center console. Nothing. He'd taken some napkins from the gas station and figured he'd use those. He took a few out of the tote bag in the backseat. Found a pen in one of the cupholders.

How to start?

Dear June. It made the most sense. Wasn't there a famous song about that? "Hey June?" He couldn't remember.

So he wrote it anyway. He started it *Dear June.* And he went on. He worked out all his thoughts that way. He couldn't spell for shit, but he tried his best. His handwriting crooked. His beaten hands shaking. He had the napkin against the wheel as he wrote. Trying to explain all his faults and fuck-ups and all the good her and his girl could make together. All the good that would come as soon as he was gone. Out of the picture. As far away from them as possible. Because he couldn't do any good for June or his girl. No matter what he tried, he failed. And this would be his final sacrifice. The last thing he could think to give her. That love and life he knew she deserved. And he didn't know if he could go on after that. That he might just take fight after fight until it really killed him. Dead in the ring. Blood on the gloves and the canvas. The dance toward the greatest dark.

He kept that last part out of the letter.

When he was done, he didn't know how to sign off. He wanted to tell June that Claudia really loved her, and in that way, he kind of loved her too. So he did. He wrote it just like that. And then he signed his name—*Lenny "Trucks" Babineaux.*

Trucks found a skinny rubber band in the center console. He rolled up the ink-filled napkins and bound them with the rubber band. Put them in the cupholder. Then he looked at Claudia. A pretty sleeping angel. His love. He felt choked off. Such an intense sadness at the thought of having to leave her. But what else could he really do? He kissed his thumb and ran it over her brow. Adjusted her left hearing aid. He'd miss her. God, he'd miss her.

Trucks righted the car and drove on. He caught the interstate and sped into the coming dark. The mile markers clocked by. They entered South Dakota. They were so much closer. Traffic was low. The more tired he got, the more nervous he became.

He saw flashing lights on the side of the road. A pulled-over speeder. The cop looked at Trucks as he drove by. He swore he did. Or maybe he imagined it? Trucks watched the whirring red-and-blue lights in the rearview. Saw them shrink as he drove on. Still. He had a nagging feeling. A fear he'd be followed.

He couldn't stop yawning. He was exhausted and losing steam. A sharp pain struck his head. Like a crack to the skull. He reached up and rubbed his aching temple.

Up ahead. A speed trap? So late in the evening? It was dark now. It was perfect dark. Was that a web of police cars ahead? All those circling lights. What was he seeing?

Trucks was afraid. Not of getting caught or arrested. He was afraid his girl wouldn't get the life she deserved. He couldn't have that. They weren't going to catch him.

They were just outside of Spearfish. He saw a sign up ahead for a side highway. He quickly took the exit and edged onto the old two-lane road. It was slick and icy. He pressed on as his body started to give to the weight of sleep.

He swerved off the road and suddenly woke. He righted the vehicle and shook his head. Everything was coming in blurs and stretched light.

He swerved off the road again. He kept hold of the wheel and got them back on the highway. It was cold and icy. That had to be the cause. It wasn't him. He was all right. He was holding up. His head hurt. So there was that. But he was doing okay. He slapped himself in the face to stay alert. But he kept blinking.

Black to light to black to light to black to light.

Then he lost control of the car in a whirl of shapes. He was seeing all kinds of colors.

He was seeing. He was seeing. He wasn't seeing.

THE BADLANDS MYTHOLOGY

Trucks looked up at the dark, empty sky as he walked along. He had his girl in his arms. Blood trickling down his forehead. The car wrecked and far behind them. His mind a mess.

"There are no stars," he said. "There are wars of fists and the lives that men make."

He could hear his footfalls in the hard-packed snow. Feel his tight-throated breaths.

"We're near the Badlands," he said. "It's where we are, baby. We're out there, you and me. You hear the crunching? That's us moving, little baby. That's us."

He breathed hard. The air stung. He took another big breath.

"You wanna have a look at the ridges? They're famous. I heard people talk about them when I was a kid. Wondered for years if there was any good out in those Badlands. Probably coyotes and prairie dogs and antelope dancing around and things. I don't know. Jesus. I don't know. But hey, do you wanna take a look up there? You can see the ridges. They're way out there, but even under all this dark, you can see them. Believe me about how you can see them."

Claudia didn't move. She was limp in his arms.

"You're tired, I know. But you understand we have to

keep going. Only one place we need to be, and we're getting there, little baby. We're damn sure getting there. Moving all the time. Making good progress. That's what these boots are for. People write songs about it. We're going. We're walking, my little girl. You little, delicate thing. We're sure as shit walking. Maybe have a look at the rocks, huh? They're not so bad. You're not so bad out there, you goddamn Badlands! We're making it. You're not stopping us. Nothing's goddamn stopping us. Hey, I'll tell you about them like I promised. Keep nodding off. I'll tell you. Then you can dream about them. I'll tell you and you can have this picture of the big dark rocks in your dream, okay?"

He staggered but kept his footing. They were alone on the bare highway.

"I'm not so good at describing things, but I'll try. I'm trying for you, okay? They're nothing but these big ridges. So you won't have to be scared of them. Remember that. But they sparkle with snow when the sun's out. Little flakes of gold packed in the hills. And I don't really see any trees out there. Picture it without trees, okay? I know you'll probably miss the trees. But there are other things. Like the rocks. Big and gray and jagged. All those ridges. But don't imagine them like that. Think of them soft and smooth for when you walk on them someday. Something delicate. Like how you'd be kind of walking on other planets. Yeah. That's probably what it is, I think. The Badlands dropped here from outer space, probably. Broke off some other planet way out there and landed here so many thousands of years ago. And it scared the shit outta the local tribes back then so they called

it *bad* because of that. Because they didn't really know what
it was. And people are always afraid of the things they don't
know. So they called the lands bad. But there's no bad out
here. Just another part of the world, you know? And there
isn't anything like trees out there. So don't think of it with
trees, okay?"

Every few feet he stumbled. And grew colder. His mind
aching and more delirious. His body shivering so hard, so
much closer to that final dark.

"But the animals, they. They survive still. Cross great dis-
tances to find food. Like hope. Nuts and grass and berries
and twigs. Eat it right off the ground. Even on cold nights.
Like this. Oh man. Hey. A herd of. Of buffalo. Of all things,
right? They're crossing the road. Fluffy wings slapping in the
wind. Sounds like bells. Wish you could hear it, little one.
Wish you could see it with me."

He looked down at her pale face. Tried to steady her as he
walked so he could kiss her forehead. But he was too shaky
and weak to reach. His condition rapidly worsening.

He relented and kept on.

"But keep. Keep sleeping, my girl. It's okay. Dream on.
But hey. I heard you can pet them. When you see them.
Because. Because they aren't bad. Or anything. The winged
buffalos. Hey. And you know. You know. Hey. Now that
I think. I think. Nobody knows. Why they're called the
Badlands. Because they're. Not. Okay? There's nothing bad.
At all. Out there. So don't think. Don't think bad. When
you think of that. Okay? Or when you. Think. Think of
us. Walking like this. All we've been. Been through. There's

nothing really. Bad. Out there. Okay? So. So don't think. Don't. Don't think. Of the world. Like that. It's just. Just the world. See? There's nothing to. Fear. There's just. There's us. There's. Us. There's. The road. And. And. There is. There is."

JONATHAN STARKE is a former bodybuilder and boxer. He has traveled through sixty countries, hitching along the way. His stories and essays have been published in many magazines and literary journals, including *The Sun*, *Missouri Review*, *Threepenny Review*, *North American Review*, *Michigan Quarterly Review*, *Greensboro Review*, *Gettysburg Review*, *Shenandoah*, and *Brevity*. He is the founder of *Palooka*, an international literary journal. *You've Got Something Coming* is his first novel.